When You Lose It All

Arti Solanki

ISBN: 978-1-959392-09-5

Dedication

The aim of having this book written is to give strength to those who have lost their loved ones during COVID-19.

I dedicate this book to all the loved ones we lost due to COVID-19

Acknowledgment

I appreciate the efforts put forth by some people very close to me who helped me accomplish this goal. I feel this immense gratitude to God Almighty, my creator. I feel thankful to my parents. Mom, thank you for being there for me. I pray that your soul forever rests in peace.

Dad! Thank you for being my biggest hero and my greatest role model.

I feel immense gratitude for my husband for making me come back to life again.

I thank my friends who are always there to care.

CONTENTS

Dedication iii

Acknowledgment iv

About the Author.. vi

Preface.. ix

Chapter 1: The Beginning of a New Journey...........1

Chapter 2: The Baby Shower 11

Chapter 3: An Excruciating Pain............................18

Chapter 4: The Wait 25

Chapter 5: An Early Visit.......................................34

Chapter 6: The Moment of Truth 42

Chapter 7: The Dark Days......................................52

Chapter 8: A Double Tragedy 57

Chapter 9: The Self-isolation Days 63

Chapter 10: A Difficult Farewell 69

Chapter 11: The Positive Side of the Story 81

Chapter 12: Another Goodbye 85

Chapter 13: A Life of Love and Loss...................101

About the Author

Arti Solanki was born into a beautiful family and raised by grandparents who were a blessing in her life and extremely important to her. Since her parents worked very hard, she spent most of her time with her grandparents, watching movies/TV programmes.

Being the only child, Arti Solanki was very spoilt, always showered with love and happiness. She had the best childhood, which she remembers very well.

Arti Solanki has been blessed with the greatest soulmate who always understands and supports her. He is her rock, and she knows that her mother left content, knowing she has left her in good hands.

The names have been changed in the chapters for the family's privacy. Following pseudonyms have been used for the family members.

Angela Shaw, to be recognised as the late mother of Ava Scott. Angela Shaw also had pet names; Hansi, Honey B, Mamma bear, Mamma Oleg, and Maju.

Recognising the late daughter of Ava Scott as Faith, who couldn't spend more time with her loved ones.

Robin Shaw is to be recognised as the father of Ava Scott.

Scott Jacobs, to be recognised as the husband of Ava Scott, who made her believe in living the life again despite all odds.

All proceeds of this book will be going to charity to help the children in India.

Preface

When You Lose It All is a memoir covering the struggles of life and death during the pandemic. The world has unexpectantly been taken up by a whirlwind of chaos as everything has turned upside down and a new order of things has taken over. Depression and anxiety are now very common occurrences.

The author of this book faced a difficult pregnancy and a complicated delivery, followed by the entire family contracting COVID-19. Thus, this story depicts the adversities faced by a family in such unprecedented times. It covers the emotional trauma experienced by them as they lose significant members of the family.

Facing the reality of the loss of loved ones is not easy, and through her words, the author aptly conveys the extent of her hardships, something that many can resonate with since the whole world is captivated by the deadly virus. The virus has not only taken lives but has disturbed people on an emotional level.

A true tale of tough times and a representation of courage and hope, this book takes you through the author's journey of facing the worst and learning how to get up again. After darkness, just as the sun rises again, we too must learn to go on.

Chapter 1
The Beginning of a New Journey

The moon had a distinctly brighter glow that night; it almost felt like it had sparks flying around it. I could hear the soft chirping of the crickets that dwelled in the dense waves of the bright autumn orange leaves of the oak tree peeking through my bedroom window. They say that the world conspires against pessimistic minds; your world starts falling apart when you consistently focus on the darker side of the picture. But at this moment, all I could see was a multitude of stars shining up above and glowworms twinkling outside, as if the entire world was cherishing the moment. The vibe was unlike any other I had ever had throughout my days, and I don’t think anything could ever bring that joyful moment back.

My eyes shined brighter than diamonds; I couldn’t hold back my tears as I wept in joy. Thirty-four-year-old me hopped on the wooden flooring out of excitement like a toddler. I just couldn’t hold my anticipation, I felt like wanting to explode like confetti in a billion pieces, and my husband felt no different. I had never seen him grin from ear to ear apart from the day of our wedding seven years ago. I held his hand as we cheerfully danced around the room in our PJs, "Show it to me; I want to get a look at it myself," Scott finally exclaimed in delight.

I handed over the pregnancy strip to him, and he sunk his face into the strip for a while and lost his smile. He stared at it with utmost concentration until, finally, his expressionless face rose and looked straight into my eyes. Within no time, his hands grasped me by the shoulders and pulled me in his arms. I could hear his soft cries as my face rested on his broad chest, and we went silent for a few seconds. "I just can't believe it, Ava, this is all just so beautiful and amazing and..., and everything just seems perfect," Scott said, as his voice cracked from the excitement. "I'm finally going to be a father! Thank you, Lord!" We heard a knock on our bedroom door, "Is everything okay in there? We heard loud noises downstairs," it was my parents. Without a second thought, I immediately flew towards the door and unlocked it to find the worried faces of my Mom and Dad as they stood outside the door.

I leapt into my mother's arms with excitement, "Mum, guess what?" – I said, as my hug grew tighter – "I took the pregnancy test, and it came back positive!" In no time, my Mum's worried expressions transitioned to a euphoric state as she hugged me back. It was not long before we all broke into joyful laughter. My family was thrilled; I could almost sense the love and positive emotions floating in the room. I couldn't have wished for anything more from my life that night.

The very next day, we booked ourselves an appointment with a general physician first thing in the morning. We got done with all of the tests without any delays to confirm my pregnancy and to check if everything was in place. All the tests came back positive, and we all heaved a sigh of relief. Amongst us all, my Mum seemed the most delighted by the news of my pregnancy. Her long-awaited dream of having a grandchild, which she started mentioning in my teenage years, was finally coming to life.

And oh did we celebrate the rest of that week like there was no tomorrow. Scott went ahead and planned us all a grand vacation to make the most of our moment since we didn't get to spend a whole lot of family time together, and almost all of us were always busy with our jobs and tight schedules. My mother has always been one of a kind; although she was extremely wise and mature, even at her current age, she still had a child trapped inside her. Since my childhood, I've always been an adventure enthusiast and loved exploring and experiencing new things, no matter how daring they were.

At first, my Mum was always sceptical about stepping out of her comfort zone, but being the only child, I was able to convince her to do weird and crazy things with me. Looking at my friends' parents,

I would often question myself if Mum was even my actual mother since I never saw that typical motherly figure in her. She would become my best friend when I needed relationship advice in my high school days. I'd find my Mum standing beside me whenever I needed assistance with girly fashion problems in my teens. I pretty much found myself rushing to my Mum for assistance in any situation I'd come across, and I don't think I was ever able to grow out of depending on my Mum for almost everything.

At this point, I was pretty much in shock as the hard blows of wind hit hard on my face. The headphones on my head blocked out the loud whooshing noise of the helicopter blades cutting through the wind. I looked out the window at the enormous skylines as we soared a thousand feet above Central London. How in the world did I even end up here? "If you look to your right, you could see King Henry's Mound where it is believed that King Henry the eighth himself witnessed the signal from the Tower of London for his wife's execution." I could hear the pilot speaking through my headphones. Scott sat in the front seat next to the pilot, and I found myself sitting in between my parents. I looked to my right and found my mother with her eyes shut tight; she had acrophobia, a fear of heights. Yet again, I was able to work my magic to convince her on a tour of London in a helicopter. I gently held her hand to comfort her, and she slightly opened her eyes to look towards me and gave me a weak smile.

I could not even keep track of all the amazing food we had and the places we visited. Museums, the beach, amusement parks, we did it all. We dined in some of the finest restaurants in all of London, some of which had absolutely breathtaking views. Scott did end up exceeding our budget in the end, which I could obviously tell being a professional financial analyst, but the memories we made were all pretty much worth it. We returned exhausted from our week-long vacation, but all of us managed to return to our normal lives. Since the insurance company where I worked was only a twenty-minute drive away from our home, I did not call off from work and got back to my job the very next day.

The 29th of January marked the day that everything started going south for London. Our first two patients with COVID-19 were confirmed, and the government immediately issued precautionary measures to contract the spread of the deadly virus. Initially, we did not pay much attention to the fatal pandemic since it was still a fairly developing story, and the UK did not have any registered cases as of yet. However, news of the first confirmed cases took me by shock because it had barely been a month since I had found out about my pregnancy.

People in general expect a newly married couple to have a child within the first two years of marriage. We were no exception to this as we would constantly be questioned about our baby, which in a way kept pressurising us to have a child. However, Scott and I decided that we were not going to let other people decide what was best for us, and we would wait for the right time to have a child. We struggled and fought against these social norms for seven whole years of our marriage until we made our big decision, and I was not going to let anything come in between my unborn child and me.

It was not long before the COVID-19 virus started spreading like wildfire across London. The number of cases dangerously skyrocketed by February, and the government started implementing partial lockdowns. I was terrified by the virus, not for myself, but for the sake of my baby. I would read up on the deadly effects the virus was having on people and how it affected pregnancy throughout the globe. This completely terrified me, and I was not going to risk anything at all that would affect my long-awaited child.

The first month of the pandemic felt as if the world was ending. All of London observed a strict lockdown. I spoke to my manager and told him that under no condition would I be working before the virus is completely eliminated because I could risk the well-being of my baby due to my job. They were pretty much understanding and issued me a temporary suspension from my duties until further notice. I strictly followed every little guideline issued by the government, including the regular use of masks and gloves, as well as disinfectants to clean every nook and corner of the house. Since I was at home, I used up my spare time to read up on whatever new precautionary measures were issued as the doctors studied the virus, and I did everything I could to protect my family. My family has always been supportive of me and has respected my opinions, and due to my pregnancy, everyone tried their best to stay as safe as possible.

We did, however, leave one little loophole in building a perfect defensive fort against the virus, and that was my Mum's job. My mother has always been extremely active and did everything by herself. She did not like asking others to do her work for her, and she was always afraid of the idea of being dependent on others. That's probably the only reason she continued to work at the supermarket: to avoid her bones from getting rusty and to maintain her financial independence.

It took me a good amount of time to explain to Mum how dangerous the virus was and how easily it contracts from person to person. Since she took the bus to her work and came in contact with many people at the overcrowded supermarket, she was highly susceptible to the virus. What scared me even more was that the virus was strictly dangerous for both young infants and the elderly since they have weaker immune systems. At first, Mum completely declined my request for her to stay home, and she continued to go to the supermarket every day. Since she continued working at the supermarket, I found myself avoiding my very own mother, and it felt like the most terrible thing in the world. I would not enter the kitchen when Mum was working there because part of me was scared that I would somehow catch the virus through my Mum, and that would put the life of my unborn child in danger.

She did not want to be bound at home and enjoyed going out and working, but soon enough, she realised that I was avoiding her and did not like that. As the statistics of the infected people started to skyrocket, I was finally able to convince her to stay home for her own sake as well as for her family's sake.

As days and weeks passed, our house felt no less than a prison cell. We completely minimised stepping out of the house. Scott was strictly the only one who would go out to get the groceries and medicines from the supermarket that was only five blocks away from our house. Even after taking extreme caution, all of us made it a habit to sanitise and wash ourselves several times a day.

Scott worked as a project manager for EPAM and was allowed to work from home through his computer, which kept him busy. Mum, on the other hand, was pretty much disturbed from staying at home since she did not have much to do apart from looking after the kitchen or doing house chores. Even though I was only 2 months into my pregnancy at this point, my family treated me like a highly fragile piece of glass that would break if touched. They wouldn't let me do anything around the house, and they made me feel like a princess throughout my pregnancy.

The modern ways of London were not able to dry out my Mum's traditional values. Every day she would come up with a new method of mixing up a bunch of herbs or spices to make something that was supposed to make my child healthier or fairer. Even though some of the edible things she would make to help me almost made me throw up, I didn't want to hurt her feelings and managed to gobble up whatever she threw at me. Since Mum was doing most of the cooking in the house, she made extra healthy meals for the entire family that were not always as tasty, but the entire family changed their ways and did not complain about the food to support me in taking a well-balanced diet. At times she would even go the extra mile to make visually appealing platters that would make up for their lack of taste.

The doctor advised me to take many vitamins and supplements, and my husband ensured that I took my meds on time every day. Scott found many different workout videos targeted towards pregnant women, and every night, we played the videos on the television and followed the exercises together. Even though not once did Scott leave my side when I needed him, the extra care and love I received from him during my pregnancy was just too overwhelming.

My family went out of the way for me to have a seamless pregnancy. Up to a certain extent, we all made our efforts and sacrificed our ways to adapt to the new changes. One good that the pandemic did do us, however, was to give us all more time to spend with each other. My family was essentially great at making the most of any situation. Where most people would whine about being trapped at home all day, we would spend our time playing board games or cards together. We enjoyed spending time with each other, and the upcoming member of the family just added to our family's blessings. To this day, I treasure each and every one of those moments more than anything, and I would give up everything I have to witness those cheerful blessed faces one last time.

Chapter 2
The Baby Shower

A mother knows just how beautiful every moment of the nine-month journey is; when her baby moves inside her womb. It is as beautiful for her as when she is finally able to hold her child in her arms. The period of pregnancy is the only time of a person's life when they are as close to their mother as they can get. Since the baby is isolated and is only able to interact with the mother in this period, a special bond develops between the child and the mother. It is truly magical. The moments my family and I spent with my baby were no less than a fantasy.

Fast forward to August, I was already seven and a half months into the pregnancy. Surprisingly enough, the excitement of my family and me only kept increasing as I started to develop a bigger bump in my belly. I could tell how excited everyone was for the upcoming member of our small family as each time someone would come across me in the house, their eyes would shift from my face towards my belly, and almost immediately, they would smile. The joy those cherished faces brought to me was like nothing else. I was glad to know that my child was bringing so much happiness to our family without even being physically present. I simply couldn't imagine how beautiful life would become for us once the child was born and grew up.

My family's happiness for my child did not end with their cheerful faces. They were doing so much not only for the baby but also for me that I already felt like a queen. Even though I was still a few months away from delivery, Mum had already started shopping for her grandchild. Clothes, toys, shoes…she bought everything! Since most of the physical stores were closed and we did not step out of the house as much because COVID was spreading like wildfire at this point, she did all her shopping online, and there was a new package on the doorstep every other day.

But things did not only stop at adorable mittens and baby bibs. We went far and beyond what you would normally expect from a family that was expecting. There was no way Mum and Dad were going to miss out on this opportunity to call every person in the world to our house and share our happiness with the people we love. I was actually quite expecting a huge celebration because we loved inviting people over to our house. We waited for public holidays or traditional days as an excuse to invite all of our friends and relatives to our humble little home. Dad was often the one who would suggest get-togethers and would plan out everything, especially the food, which 7 out of 10 times would be BBQ because he loved showing off his super deluxe BBQ grill.

Even though COVID was at its peak, Mum and Dad just couldn't resist the temptation of celebrating the moment with other people. That was when Dad couldn't hold it in anymore and finally let it out, "Look, I know it's COVID and everything, and we're trying our best to stay clear from any unwanted diseases, but that doesn't mean we would stop living our lives." Mum immediately cut him off and added, "Yes! Your Dad's right. We're not going to let some virus stop us from making the most of this time. You're not going to get this time back again, you know, a small get-together won't harm anyone." I was sceptical of what Mum and Dad thought because I didn't want to risk anything at such a critical time of the pandemic. I expected Scott to jump in and show a little wisdom which he did, well, kind of… "I'm sorry, Mom, but a small get-together won't just cut it. We're going to throw a grand baby shower for Ava. I'll call in the event planners to make a booking for this week." Scott's words of wisdom almost made me want to bang my head in the wall, but I just nodded and agreed to the whole thing. "Okay, okay, but on the condition that there will be NO compromises on health safety," to which everyone reasonably agreed.

Scott pretty soon got busy with the event planners, and Mum got started with sending out the invitations. We wanted to keep everything to a bare minimum, but after we started out with the preparations, we may have gone a little overboard. Mum's guest list kept on growing with each passing day, the event planners kept convincing Scott to expand his budget a little further to get everything to be perfect, and of course, Dad was not going to miss out on the opportunity to pull out his BBQ grill. He bought all the supplies for a delightful BBQ.

On the 23rd of August, the morning vibes were really something else. I woke up tired from staying up late helping everyone with all the preparations, but that didn't stop me from having butterflies in my stomach just thinking about my baby. The team from the event planners came over early to start setting up the house for the baby shower and finalise the decorations. We had decided on a white coloured theme for the baby shower to keep the decorations at a minimal and decent level. All of the arrangements were made in our yard. I was quite surprised at what an exceptional job the event planners did with the decorations. Beautiful flower bouquets, crystal white chairs, the buffet tabled stretched out across the yard with all sorts of delicious sandwiches, sausages, burgers, salads, and fruits. There was a special separate section set up for the humongous gender reveal cake Scott surprised me with. It was a sight to look at; four layers of heavenly white cream shined in the bright sunlight, beautiful red edible roses climbed on the sides with an adorable little baby figure crawling on the top. I couldn't have asked for anything more.

Scott specifically asked the manager of the event planning company to make special precautionary arrangements to keep everything strictly hygienic. The team wore masks and gloves as they worked on setting everything up in the house. We had sanitisers placed on every corner of the yard along with a box of gloves and masks on the main entrance, and all the chairs for the guests were placed at a distance from each other.

The guests started coming in at around 4 in the evening, we made sure all the guests washed their hands and disinfected themselves before entering, and everyone cooperated. The baby shower helped me connect with old acquaintances since I had invited a couple of my friends who I hadn't been able to meet in a long time and was able to reconnect with them. Scott had also invited a bunch of his guy friends accompanied by their better halves. We also had many relatives from my parents' side, which allowed me to reconnect with them. It's times like these when we realise how important it is to keep in touch with our family, which we usually take for granted in our busy lives.

I avoided physical interactions and softly gestured away anyone who approached me for hugs or kisses because I was not going to take any risks for my baby, even for my cousins, whom I have loved and adored all my life. Since I do not have any siblings, I have spent most of my time with my cousins throughout my life, and they've never let me feel the absence of a brother or sister. They were always there for me in my ups and downs, and me having a baby was nothing different. Even after we had all grown up to have our own families, we still met like we were in our teens. Everyone was happy with my long-awaited pregnancy. I was not expecting to receive the enormous mountain of gifts from the guests that we had to set up on a separate table in the yard. Dad was having the time of his life as he prepared the juicy smoked ribs on his grill. I got so indulged and started enjoying catching up with everyone that it eliminated all the second thoughts I was having about arranging a baby shower in the pandemic.

The sun was about to set, and we all got done with the food and moved towards the main course everyone was anxiously waiting for, the big gender reveal! Scott and I had decided not to tell Mum and Dad about the gender of my baby and to surprise them with everyone else at the baby shower. Scott fetched the knife, and all the guests circled the big cake. Scott and I held the knife as we slowly and dramatically sliced into the cake. Everyone burst into cheers and laughter as we pulled out a piece that revealed a subtle baby pink colour on the inside of the cake. I was going to have a girl. Mum and Dad burst into tears of joy and pulled me into a big hug. I could see rainbows all around me, and my heart bloomed with joy that day.

We got done with the baby shower as all the guests started to leave right after sunset. Some of my cousins stayed back to help me clean up, and I later convinced them to spend the night at our place. It didn't take us long to clean up with all the extra hands we had. Scott called in the event planners to pick their decorative stuff and fixtures up. Once we got done with the cleaning, we gathered around in the living room to open up all of the presents and, oh boy, had I ever seen so many baby products at once in my life. I had a pile of baby clothes, lotions, creams, cribs, and whatnot. I was overwhelmed by all of the love attached to each gift, knowing how much the people I know cared about me.

The rest of the night was no different as we spent that entire night talking and laughing, recalling all of the dumb things we did together when we were children. The childish games we played like musical chairs and pass-the-parcel just made everything twice as fun. My cousins gathered up many baby products that I got in my gifts and mixed them up in a large bowl; they blindfolded me and made me guess each product by just touching them. It was not until six in the morning that we all got super tired and finally decided to call it a day. We all crashed on the couches and the floor carpet. I lay on one of the couches, reminiscing my day with a smile on my face as my drowsy eyes slowly blinked till I finally fell asleep.

Chapter 3
An Excruciating Pain

No matter how dense the clouds, there always comes a time when the rain must stop; that's the way of nature. I was so deeply absorbed in all the wholesome moments of the future that I completely forgot about the present. But a part of me still holds on to the idea that clinging on to good memories and having hope in your future is still better than suffering in the present.

A week passed, and I was still not able to get over the dazzling baby shower that felt nothing short of a fantasy. Scott came back a little early from work that day, and Mum and Dad were out to visit my Aunt, so we had the whole house to ourselves and got to spend some quality time with each other. I made us some delicious grilled steaks and mashed potatoes to feast on that night. We switched off all the lights in the house, and I lit the table up with some candles for a romantic little dinner. When we got done with our cute little date at home, Scottt and I danced around the living room to some Beyoncé and Shayne Ward songs. ScottScott pulled out his camera and started taking pictures of me while I made the weirdest poses I could come up with.

We eventually got tired from acting like teenagers and

went upstairs. I rolled around the bed, laughing like a hyaena as Scott made the lamest jokes he could come up with. “Alright, alright, what kind of emotions does a nose feel?” asked Scott, “I don’t know, what?” I replied while I kept giggling. “Nos-talgia,” Scottexclaimed as I burst out laughing again. Scotts stupid humour was one thing I could never get over and appealed to me from the first day we met. He had this power to come up with the dumbest jokes in any situation that allowed him to get out of the tensest situations by just laughing it off. Once my stomach started hurting from laughing so hard I told Scott to put on a nice relaxing movie, and the best thing he could think of was Narnia because Scott had a thing for highly aggressive action movies where they just blew everything up. It had been a while since I had such a magical time with Scott, and I couldn’t have asked for more.

Deep inside me, even after the wonderful moments I had for the past few months, I still had this tiny feeling hiding in a corner that soon, a strong gust of wind would blow away all these rainbows from above my head. We both passed out with the TV still turned on, and I dozed off with my head rested on Scott’s chest and his arms wrapped around my shoulders. It wasn’t long before my sleep was disturbed as I started to move restlessly on the bed and felt a sharp sting of pain in my stomach that slowly grew stronger and stronger. I kept rolling on the bed from side to side with my eyes shut in a failed attempt to fall asleep and ignore the pain but with no luck. I didn't want to worry Scott as he was completely worn out and slept peacefully beside me. I was worried and terrified that something was wrong.

The pain gradually grew stronger; it felt as if someone was punching me in the belly with their bare fists. My face twisted and turned until I could no longer bear it. I shot up and sat straight on the bed. The staggering pain was not just the after-effects of some spicy Mexican food; something was definitely not right. My suspicions were proved right as I pushed away the blanket to find stains of blood on my pyjamas. "Scott, wake up. I think something's wrong," I said as I nudged him. Scott immediately got up and was terrified from seeing the bloodstains on my PJs and the bed. "Oh good gracious! You're bleeding. What happened?" I looked at him and told him I had no clue, and I was in extreme pain. Scott went downstairs to fetch me a glass of water. I chugged the glass because my throat had completely dried off from panting like an Olympic runner. "Scott, the pain is killing me. I feel like someone's hit me with a dagger or something. Please do something." I cried. "I think we need to consult a doctor immediately," he said as he reached for his phone on the table.

Scott frantically dialled up the maternity ward and quickly explained the entire situation. The doctor told Scott to calm down and to get me on the phone. "Okay, sweetie, my name is Cindy, can you please tell me exactly where you're feeling the pain?" the doctor questioned me in a gentle tone. "I think it's mostly in my lower abdomen, but I'm not exactly sure because my entire body is aching right now," I told her as my voice cracked from the pain. The doctor had a very comforting tone, "I do understand that, but you need to remain calm for me, okay?" she reassured me as she assessed that I was too worried from my tone. "It's probably just the contractions, and those are actually normal during the third trimester of pregnancy that you're well into now," she added.

"I am literally sitting in a pool of blood right now, and that doesn't seem normal," I was now getting anxious. "Ava dear, I know that you're worried looking at the blood, but that tends to happen during pregnancy, and it is completely normal. Could you tell me the consistency of the blood and how the flow is?" I was growing more and more impatient, but I managed to stay calm throughout the conversation. "The blood is thick and has stopped flowing now, but I think I've already bled quite a lot." The doctor paused for a few seconds and replied, "Okay, I don't think we have anything to worry about here. I'll prescribe a few painkillers on text, that should help ease out the pain. It'll take a bit of time for the meds to kick in, so hang in there, but if the pain doesn't go away after a while, give me another call, okay." The doctor said and hung up.

I dropped the phone on the bed and turned towards Scott. I could see how worried he was from his expressions. I told him what the doctor said and that we shouldn't worry too much. Pregnancy is actually a step-by-step journey, and you learn as you progress through each stage. Since I was only 31 weeks and 5 days into pregnancy at this point, we hadn't really consulted with our doctor to discuss what the contractions were, so I had no idea whether this was normal or not. Scott helped me get out of the bed and assisted me towards the bathroom. I washed off all the blood from between my thighs and changed into a comfy pair of shorts. By the time I got out, Scott had fetched medicines from the first aid kit, which we thankfully had already bought as a precaution. He stood outside the bathroom with the meds and a glass of water. I stepped out and sat on the sofa to catch my breath. Scott handed over the meds, and I gulped them down. Now started the most excruciating test as I waited for the pain to diminish. It almost felt like time had stopped; every minute that went by felt like a year to me.

I lay on my bed in agonising pain; an hour flew by as we waited for the painkillers to start working but to no avail. They didn't seem to make even the slightest difference. "Honey, this pain is killing me. Please do something," I said to Scott. "I think we should give the maternity ward another call," Scott said as he dialled the phone and handed it over to me. I spoke to the same doctor again and told her that the meds didn't work and that the pain was getting worse. "Okay, I think we need to get you a stronger dose of painkillers. Try these, and hopefully, these should do the trick." She continued, "If these don't help in reducing the pain within 20 minutes, give me another call, and I'll tell you what to do, okay?" She sent a text with a prescription for the new meds, which we didn't have. Scott immediately got up and flew out of the house to fetch the painkillers. Fortunately, we have a 24/7 pharmacy just a few blocks away from our house. Pretty soon, he got back, and I took the new medicines hoping that they'd help reduce the pain now. Those twenty minutes felt like they were never going to end. The staggering pain lingered, and the new meds didn't seem to work either. I was now on the verge of crying; my entire body shivered because of the pain.

Scott called the doctor again and told her that my condition was now extremely serious, and we needed to get first aid ASAP. The doctor finally told him that he needed to bring me to the hospital for further investigation. He dropped the phone and helped me get up to take me to the hospital. Scott held my hand as we made our way downstairs to the car. I saw Mum and Dad's car parked in the driveway. "Scott… should we… let Mum and Dad know about this?" I asked Scott in a small tone as I struggled to speak because of the pain. "I think it's best if we don't right now. They're only going to get worried," Scott replied to me as he tried to calm me down. "Don't worry. You're going to be fine. We'll be back before they wake up." It was 6 in the morning, and I guess Scott made the right decision of not waking my parents up as there was no point in getting them worried in the middle of the night. I didn't bother getting dressed and walked out the door in shorts and a button-down shirt. Scott helped me get in the back of the car, and I immediately lay down. He quickly got in the driver's seat, started the car, and we zoomed off. I was still twisting and turning from the pain, but that wasn't my biggest concern at the moment. Throughout our drive to the hospital, which seemed like a never-ending journey, I only had one question in mind, "Is the baby okay?"

Chapter 4
The Wait

I sat upright with my back against the car door, panting to breathe and dripping in sweat. Scott looked at me suffocating from the rear view and pulled down the windows a bit so I could get some fresh air. Strong waves of wind flew in as Scott frantically drove faster, and our car swooshed down the highway. I glanced out at the blurred trees that flew past us, tears streaming down my face.

I was frightened, not because of the intense pain I was suffering, but because a part of me kept saying that something was just not right. We hadn't consulted our doctor to discuss the contractions yet because I had done enough research and knew that pregnancy goes through its complete cycle. I wasn't supposed to suffer such intense pain in the phase I was in.

What if I had eaten something wrong, or what if I had put too much pressure on myself from all the physical exhaustion I put myself through in the past days? I could never forgive myself if I put the life of my child in any sort of danger. But maybe I was just overthinking; I kept telling myself that my intuition was wrong and that nothing was going to happen to my baby.

I could hear faint words in the background. Scott was trying to calm me down and check on me, but his voice drained my ears, and I couldn't understand or respond to him. It was like the world around me had gone blurry. The pain was so intense that it felt like I lost consciousness, and I kind of wished that I did too if it would help drown the pain a bit, but I somehow managed to keep myself together.

Sunlight started to pour in as the sun peaked through the horizon. Scott finally pulled into the hospital driveway after a twenty-minute journey that seemed to take forever. He stopped the car in front of the gate, and a ward boy who happened to be passing by our car to enter the hospital premises saw me struggling to get out of the car. He quickly ran up to the doorway to fetch a wheelchair and came running towards the car to assist me.

"Wait, ma'am, you look like you're in an awful lot of pain," he said as he grabbed my hand to help me out. "You're in no condition to walk; I'll escort you inside." He gestured for me to sit in the wheelchair. I was struggling to breathe, yet, by now, I was convinced that there was nothing wrong with me or my child. Wheelchairs are for sick people, and there was nothing wrong with me. "I appreciate your gesture… but I think I'm going to walk in. I'm fine, thank you." I built up the strength to stand on my feet and started walking towards the entrance.

Scott left the car upfront and handed over the keys to the valet. He held my hand and helped me walk inside. We made our way towards the maternity ward. I walked towards the front desk, leaned, and squeezed onto the desk to keep myself from falling down but still managed to keep myself together, "Hi, my name's Ava. I spoke to Dr. Cindy on the phone a few minutes ago. Can you please quickly let her know that I'm here? I'm in severe pain right now." The receptionist, who looked like a scientist with her face completely covered by a plastic face mask and dressed in special anti-COVID attire, immediately pulled out some papers and handed over a urine sample bottle to me. "Ava? Oh yes, Cindy did inform me that you were coming in. I'm going to need a urine sample for some quick tests, and Andy here is going to help show you the way towards the ward."

As we started walking in, she immediately stopped Scott, who happened to be following me, and said, "Sir, I apologise, but the hospital's policy restricts attendants accompanying patients inside the wards due to COVID." Scott's expressions immediately changed. "What? My wife is in severe pain right now. She needs my assistance."

"Sir, you have nothing to worry about. Andy here will accompany your wife inside, and our team of nurses will make sure to take utmost care of her. I would really appreciate your cooperation." I turned back and held Scott's hand, "It's okay, sweetie. I'll be back before you know it. Please wait outside." Scott calmed down and said, "Alright, honey, I'll just wait here for you; please take care, and oh yes… do keep in touch with me on your phone and update me on whatever goes on, okay? Love you." I nodded in agreement and quickly turned around to walk in towards the restroom.

Given my condition, I thought, 'Why am I being asked for a sample right now? They haven't even checked me up yet.' But from all my previous visits, I guess I couldn't question that because it was a standard procedure to conduct tests during pregnancy. I somehow managed to bottle the sample and got out of the restroom to find Andy waiting outside for me.

We made our way towards the wards, but as we grew closer, I was surprised by the screeching voice of someone screaming, perhaps a woman. It grew louder and louder as we got closer to the wards. The shrill screams stung my ears and felt like they came straight from hell. The wards had three bays, and Andy led us towards the first bay from where the screams were coming from. We entered the room and were welcomed by a team of nurses and doctors that were frantically running here and there.

The bay was split in two, with four beds on each side covered with curtains around them. Two of the nurses saw us enter the ward and immediately ran towards us to assist me. They helped me walk towards one of the beds on the left. As I walked, I caught a glance over two beds on the right that partially had their curtains open, and I could see inside. That was where all the screaming was coming from. The women were in intensive labour and were screaming due to immense pain. However, I could relate to the intensity of their screams, which was in the exact amount of pain I was in, but I had somehow managed to keep myself together and was able to walk all the way into the ward without screaming like a crazy maniac.

All the doctors and nurses in the ward were dressed in COVID protective gear from top to bottom. They wore big white jumpsuits with protective headgears that shielded their faces with a plastic sheet. The nurses helped me get into the bed and immediately got down to work, assessing the condition I was in. They started to ask questions regarding my condition and the kind of pain that I felt at the moment and made notes on a pad. One of them fastened probes and straps around my belly to set up the foetal monitor and check up on the baby's heartbeat to see if she was doing okay.

As they were setting everything up, Cindy came in and asked how I was doing. "You have absolutely no idea of the immense pain I'm in right now. It almost feels like my stomach is going to explode. Please do something quickly." Cindy tried to calm me down and told me that I was absolutely fine and that they were going to run a few tests to diagnose what was causing all the pain. She directed one of the nurses to run the foetal monitor.

The machine that stood beside me started giving out readings, making beep sounds. Cindy came to my side and pointed towards the machine, saying, "See, the baby's heartbeat. We've got a perfectly normal rhythm; she couldn't be doing any better, so you've got absolutely nothing to worry about." I heaved a sigh of relief, and all of my negative thoughts immediately drained out of my head.

"Alright, Ava, now I do understand that you're going through a lot of pain at the moment, but I can't give you any painkillers to relieve the pain just yet. We've sent out your samples for tests, and once they come back, we'll continue with your treatment. Till then, I want you to hold on tight for me there, okay?" I had my eyes shut at this point as I was starting to develop a headache by now. I nodded in agreement. The screams of the two women all of a sudden grew even louder than before. "Perfect, okay, Ava, I've got two other women who are going into labour right now, and we're really short-staffed. I need to go assist them, but I'll be back as soon as your results come in. If you need anything, just ring the buzzer beside your bed, alright?" she said as she walked out of the curtain wrapped around my bed.

Scott! I had completely forgotten about him. I picked up my phone lying on the side table beside my bed. I had received around 15 messages from Scott asking if I was okay. I quickly pulled up the camera and sent Scott a picture of the foetal monitor and its readings, and gave him a call. “Scott, our baby is completely fine and has a perfectly normal heartbeat. You don’t need to worry, honey.” I said to which I heard Scott take a deep breath and cry, “Thank God! I was getting so worried. How are you doing? Did the pain die down a bit?” Scott asked. “Not really, no, I’m still in quite agonising pain, but the doctor said she needs to run a few tests before they give me the painkillers. I think this is going to take a good amount of time,” I said. “Have you told the nurses that you’re still in pain?” Scott asked me. “Yes, honey, I have. They’re busy with other patients, and they’re waiting for my test results to come back.” I told him.

“Okay, hon, try to sleep if you can so the pain can die down a bit, and you don’t need to worry about a thing, honey. I’m right here for you. They don’t have any seats outside, so I’m sitting on the staircase right outside the ward. You can tell me if you need anything, alright?” Scott said. I told him that I was fine and that it would be best if he waited for me in the car to avoid COVID contractions in the hospital. He agreed to that and waited for me in the car.

The pain was just getting to my head, and I needed something to keep my mind off of it. I kept texting Scott to distract myself, but this strategy wasn't too effective either. Almost an hour had flown by since we had left our home, and it was around 7 in the morning. That was when my phone buzzed, and I got Mum's text. She had woken up and had noticed that we were missing and was growing worried. Mum asked me where I was and if I was okay. I sent her a picture of the ward and told her about the entire situation.

Mum immediately got worried, and I tried to calm her down. Dad was probably still sleeping, so I told her not to wake him up or worry him either. I tried to convince her that we'd be back home as soon as I got the painkillers.

While I was busy texting Mum, Scott was outside sitting in the car. He felt helpless just sitting around and waiting, so he decided to make productive use of his time and started to run a Google search about my symptoms. I guess it's really important to have a decent amount of knowledge about your condition yourself, and the internet is an extraordinary place to learn everything that you're going through within a matter of minutes. As Scott dug deeper and deeper into articles, he found more about my condition and the exact symptoms that had shown up in my condition.

"Placenta abruption?" Scott said as he opened up one article after another about the disease that completely resembled my condition. As he continued to read the articles, a stream of terror took over his body. Scott got goosebumps as he continued to read the extreme dangers of the condition and how it threatened to cut off the oxygen supply of the baby, putting the life of the mother in extreme danger if it wasn't treated immediately. Scott's eyes popped wide open, and he started to shiver from learning about placenta ruptures. He frantically dialled my number to talk to me while praying that I didn't suffer from this condition. My phone kept ringing on the side table; it buzzed and kept vibrating. Scott knew something was wrong as he dialled for the third time. I wasn't replying to his texts now either; the phone kept vibrating on the table and moved slowly with each ring till it tumbled off on one side of the table and fell down. Scott was too late, and that was when my world came crashing down.

Chapter 5
An Early Visit

We're all so racked up in our own lives that we stop appreciating the people and the things we have until we're suddenly hit by an unexpected turn, pain, suffering, and that's when we start appreciating the little things we have. My hands tightly grasped the bed sheet on both sides as I sat straight. My head felt like it was about to explode from the intense pain that had grown unbearable now. All the attendants and doctors were busy with the other two ladies in labour. I tried to scream for help, but no voice came out of my mouth. My whispers for help faded out in the screams from the other two ladies.

I lost my patience and finally decided to get out of bed to call one of the doctors to help me, but just as I pushed down on the bed and tried to get my legs down, it felt like all of my insides drained out of me. A giant gush of water spilled all over the bed, and all my clothes from the waist down got wet. I was astonished at what had just happened, and I was finally able to scream my heart out from the stream of pain that went down my body. My mind completely froze as I couldn't understand what was happening with my body.

The two nurses pushed through the curtains as they immediately came running in to check up on me. One of the nurses asked me what had happened, and her eyes swayed to and fro the bed and my face. I was dripping in sweat and completely exhausted as I spoke, panting for breath, “I don’t know. I was just trying to get out of the bed, and all of a sudden, this gush of water just flowed straight out of me.” The nurses looked at each other in confusion, and one of them questioned me, “Wait, aren’t you still 7 months into your pregnancy right now?” She said as she picked up some papers lying on my bedside table. “Yes… and I have no idea why all of this is happening to me. Can someone please care to explain what’s happening with me?” I replied hastily as I was now losing my calm.

One of the nurses walked out the curtains to quickly fetch a doctor. I looked down at the bed and was astonished at the amount of water that came out of my belly. The sheets were so full of water that they started dripping down the sides. I asked the other nurse to pick my phone up, and she handed it over. There were around 15 missed calls and a dozen messages from Scott. Oh god, I completely forgot about Scott. He was probably getting worried sick and must be thinking that something had happened to me. I took a photo of the bed drowning in water and sent it to Scott.

Almost immediately, he called me up again, and I picked

his call up. "Babe! Are you okay? Why weren't you picking up my calls or replying to any of my texts? I was getting so worried about you, and what's this picture that you just sent me?" Scott frantically spoke without taking a breath. "Scott, I… I uh…" the phone slipped out of my hand and landed on the bed. I could hear Scott's faint screams calling my name from the phone's earpiece. I was in no condition to talk at this point. A doctor entered and immediately started examining me. I dropped back on the pillow, my eyes started blinking fast, and I struggled to stay awake. Was I losing consciousness, or did my body just have it with the intense pain and suffering?

"Okay, I think she's hyperventilating. We need to undress her and conduct a few examinations immediately," the doctor instructed the nurses and then turned towards me. "Ava, we've got your test results back, and I think I know what's happening to you, but you don't have to worry about a thing. Everything's going to be fine. I just want you to hang in there a little longer for me, okay?"

I was still quite aware of my surroundings. It felt as if all of my insides were being squeezed out of my body, and all I could do was scream helplessly, hoping that the doctors would figure out soon what was wrong. Scott was standing outside the ward frantically pressing the buzzer to call someone out and let him in.

But since everyone was busy looking after me, nobody attended the door.

They took my clothes off and started examining me. The baby monitor was still strapped on to me, but I couldn't see the readings. Soon enough, I heard the doctor say, "Yes, my doubts were correct; she is going into labour!" I completely froze for a second. My mind couldn't process what I had just heard. "Labour?!?!" I exclaimed. "How is that even possible? I'm still 2 months away from my delivery period. How could I be in labour?" There were just so many things happening at once that I couldn't contemplate anything. As if the physical pain was just not enough, there were just so many things that I couldn't understand that deeply disturbed my mental state. It felt like everything I've ever known was all just a lie. I was just not ready for this.

"Get the theatre ready; we have to move her in immediately. This is a critical patient. I want everything to go perfectly." The doctor was talking to the nurse while I lay down there in total confusion. I was totally alone there with these strangers telling me that I was about to give birth. "Where is my husband? I want my husband here!" I said to the doctor as a cry for help. "Ava, you don't have to worry, we're taking you to the theatre, and we've informed your husband. He's on his way." The doctor replied.

They covered me with a white sheet and started to move my bed out of the curtain. At this point, there were around five or six doctors and nurses around me, all trolleying my bed out of the ward towards the theatre. With the pain at its peak, all I could do was scream along the way. I could see the lights flashing by as I stared at the roof. I could hear a bunch of voices in my ear telling me that everything was going to be okay and I should take deep breaths, but then I heard someone say, "Oh, there's your husband, Ava." I couldn't lift my head up to see Scott but knowing the fact that Scott was beside me gave me some comfort that someone I could trust was beside me at this time. I kept staring at the roof until the last light flashed in my eyes as I was pushed through the doors into complete darkness.

The room was very dimly lit. Giving birth is a frightening process when it's your first time. The pain takes control of your entire body, and the only thing you can think of during labour is a way to stop the pain. The doctors strapped a bunch of patches to monitor the baby's condition as well as mine. Premature childbirths are apparently life-threatening for both the mother and the child. So, not only did the doctors have to constantly monitor how the baby was doing, but they also had to keep me alive at the same time. We were at high risk, and there was an absolutely zero margin of error.

One of the doctors started the ultrasound and got shocked when he saw the baby on the screen. “Sir, I think we have a problem. We may have a breech birth here.” She exclaimed. “We cannot risk any complications. How are we doing on the baby’s heartbeat?” another doctor asked. “We don’t have a heartbeat on the foetal… ECV is not an option right now; we need to get her out immediately.” I heard one of the doctors say, and it was at that moment that my world completely turned upside down.

“Okay, we have a leg coming out. We don’t have time to flip her over. We’re going to have to swiftly pull her out.” One of them said. Another doctor came over my shoulder, “Ava, I want you to take deep breaths and help me with this, okay? Just remember, tighten up your lower muscles like a fist and then relax them, simple.” She explained to me.

I took deep breaths and did as I was instructed. I pushed with all my might for my baby’s sake. I wasn’t going to stop pushing till the very last drop of energy was drained out of me. I wanted my baby to live, even if it took my own life in the process. Those were the longest twenty minutes of my life that I fought on the line between life and death.

“8:47. Female. Mother is doing well.” The doctor said as she held the baby in her arms and let out a sigh of relief. I had completely drained myself. It felt as if I had run up a mountain and just wanted to faint, but before I passed out in a deep sleep, I saw the doctor's expressions change immediately.

"She's not breathing, and we don't have a pulse. Looks extremely weak. We need to shift her to an incubator ASAP." I heard the doctor say, and that was the last glance I saw of my child. Before I could even get a chance to even touch her, I passed out.

The doctors took her out into another ward next door. They tried giving her mild chest compressions because they couldn't inflict too much force due to her weak state, but that didn't help them at all. They tried giving a small dose of epinephrine to kick-start her heartbeat, but that didn't seem to make any immediate effects either. The baby was getting no pulse, and the doctors almost thought that they had lost her. She couldn't breathe, and they had to put her on a ventilator. My eyes slowly blinked as I came back to life. There was a nurse standing on my right and Scott standing on my left. "Babe! You're back. Oh, thank God, I was getting so worried. How are you feeling?" Scott said.

"I'm fine," I said as I tried to lift myself off the bed. "Where is my baby?" I asked. "Ma'am, please lie down. You need to get some rest." The nurse said. "Honey, you need to relax; our baby is fine, the doctors said that she is just very weak and was having trouble breathing, so she's on a vent right now, but we'll be able to see her very soon once her condition settles down a bit."

"My child is on a ventilator?!?!" My little mind just couldn't function anymore at this point. I couldn't even understand if any of this was real. I only wished that all of this would be nothing more than just a dream and hoped it would all end soon and I'd wake up because I couldn't bear any of this. I had never thought that my perfect little life would get so messed up in a jiffy. All the perfect dreams I had seen for my daughter were just vanishing in thin air, and I couldn't keep myself together. What kind of a nightmare is this where I couldn't see my own child?

Chapter 6
The Moment of Truth

There are moments in your life when God tells you that no matter how much you plan and take things for granted, sometimes you are hit with a sudden jerk. My whole world turned upside down in the past few months, and today I was lying in a hospital bed where I was greeted with the worst nightmares of my life.

The doctors announcing that my newborn child was on a ventilator was enough to tear my soul apart. My whole body, already under post labour trauma, went through the excruciating pain no mother would have imagined going through. After 7 long years of waiting, when God blessed us with this angel, my husband and I had to be tested with such difficult and unbearable pain. I was already numb due to the epidural the doctors administered on my shoulder. I had no energy left. The pain of knowing that my child was not in good shape, of whom I could just get a glimpse after birth in the morning, was agonising. She was already struggling for her life. It seemed as if it were just yesterday that we were announcing my pregnancy. My whole body was struggling to get up from the bed and get hold of my child lying in the incubator with a ventilator attached to her. Finally, I got to have the second glimpse of my baby late at 11 pm that night.

All that unfolded like thunder, and a non-seasonal blizzard, swept me away in the middle, where I was still trying to comprehend what had just happened to me. My senses were completely frozen, and I was in extreme agony where nothing was in my control. Delivering after 31.5 weeks of pregnancy, it was difficult to comprehend the truth when the nurse said, "Your baby is doing very poorly as she was born without a heartbeat."

We didn't get to see our baby for several hours. I kept inquiring what had happened to my baby; nobody gave me a clear picture, all they had to say was, "She is in safe hands." I asked my husband, "Is this for real?" My husband and I were going through the hardest of times in our life. Our dreams seemed to be falling apart. I was wondering and asking myself, "What went wrong? Did I do something during my pregnancy that led to such complications?" I was totally in disbelief.

After delivering my daughter, the nurses and the doctor took her to another room within no time, and I was left alone. I was feeling anxiety at its highest level. Due to COVID, the hospital was not allowing anybody within its proximity apart from the patients. Scott was waiting outside. I called him to come inside and asked the doctors to at least let my husband be with me at this time of distress. Due to COVID, all people entering the hospital were tested for their temperatures, and Scott was tested as well. Unfortunately, he had a 37.5 degrees Celsius temperature, and 37 degrees is considered normal. He was just 0.5 degrees above the normal temperature, but the doctors did not allow him to enter unless his COVID test result came back negative. He was tested immediately for the virus and was asked to go back until his report was clear. The doctors responded, "He has to go home until we get his report, and there is absolutely nothing we can do about it." This unbearable pain of not knowing exactly what had happened to my newborn baby and how it happened was taking a great toll on my sanity. I could not bear staying over there anymore and asked the nurses and the doctors to discharge me as soon as possible and let me go home. I was going insane, staying in the hospital where my pain and stress increased with every passing minute.

I could not understand what was going on, and I kept asking them, "Is she alright?" With all the COVID emergencies, I was totally clueless about the real scenario and my newborn baby's condition. My husband and I were shifted to another room. I opened up in front of my husband and complained about the disturbing situation that we were in. There was nothing wrong with my pregnancy throughout. I did not know much about Scott's situation, but he was surely going through a lot. I could see the paleness on his face, and the care in his worried heart was radiating very clearly through his eyes. He had to leave and go home or stay outside in the parking lot. I became angry with the doctors, who told Scott to go home. I told them, “I cannot go home, and now you are saying that my husband has to leave.” I was in dire need of genuine support, and Scott was the person whom I needed the most at that time. I wanted to run away from this place just to be together with him and my family to share our pain together. At the same time, my husband comforted me by saying, “We will remain in contact through WhatsApp.” Anything coming out of Scott was a big patch of relief to the pain that I was in. I was once again left in the darkness of my solitude to face the entire trauma by myself.

I was so tired and exhausted that I just completely lost my patience and told the staff that I could not stay there as I would go completely insane. I told them, “I do not have any support except this stranger midwife who does not know me and cannot understand what I need.” In the meanwhile, Scott and I were constantly chatting over the phone. I also tried to push for his early COVID test results so that he could come and pick them up at the earliest. I also wanted him to come and see our newborn daughter.

I requested the midwife to help get my husband’s COVID test result so that he could see our little angel himself. While I was waiting for him to come, I went to see our daughter once again, who looked nothing but a miracle to me at that moment. She was not breathing herself; however, she was lying inside the incubator with the ventilator on. It was so painful for me to see my newborn in this position. Although I had severe pain in my body, the adrenaline effect that I was going through eradicated the feeling of all the pain within me. I wanted to hold my newborn daughter and stay with my husband. The midwife somehow managed to get hold of his negative result. I am still very thankful to her for the favour she did for us. The sleepless nights, the after-effects of an epidural, and the stress and anxiety building up in my mind were all too much to endure alone. Thankfully, Scott came in around eleven at night, and we both sat next to our daughter. I prayed with all my heart and wondered how this could happen to us? I was trying to figure out where I had gone wrong.

Then the nurse told me, “Sister, sometimes things get out of our control without any warning sign. We do not know, but such things do happen.” I inquired, “Is this what pregnancy is? My whole pregnancy was perfect; nothing was wrong.” There was a huge fight going on inside my mind. I was wondering, what did I do wrong? I hardly ate fried food and drank ginger beer just twice. I ate carefully, only healthy food. While I was floating and revolving around the waves of these thoughts, I thought that I needed to be well for my daughter now. My thoughts took me to the realm of the situation and told me that I should go home and rest for my child’s sake and come back fresh in order to take good care of my daughter. I was preparing to go home and rest and was about to leave with a catheter still on when a doctor budged in and asked me for my urine sample before I went home. I was very disappointed to hear that. It was especially difficult at that time since I just did not want to do anything but go home.

The doctor asked me for a specific amount in mL of the urine sample. I drank tons and tons of water, gave my urine sample, and finally left for home. It was a huge relief to be back with my family at home. This was all I wanted since this was the best form of comfort. I was still under the effect of the epidural; hence I slept during the night and woke up the next morning. My mother was leaving for work as it was Monday (a working day). I met her briefly in the evening that day. The next day after waking up, I felt that my pain was still not completely over. There was a huge hollowness within my soul with my daughter in the hospital on a ventilator. Nothing seemed to be the same. My father was home, as it was his day off from work. When I saw my father, I completely broke down in front of him and could not hold my emotions. I started crying my heart out and wanted to keep all my worries and fright in front of him. At that moment, everything seemed a blur. My father was also heartbroken to see me in tears. He assured me that our daughter was at one of the best hospitals in the city; they would take good care of her, and she would be home with us in no time.

Scott and I visited our daughter in the afternoon. My newborn baby was still kept inside an incubator. After seeing my daughter, I again started wondering where I had gone wrong. She was such a soft and tiny little baby. I was due on the 27th of October and gave birth two months earlier in August. She was a premature baby, and the doctors said that such complications occurred without any reason. However, I could not stop myself from thinking about the mistakes I might have made unknowingly. My emotions revolved between guilt and thinking if it was God's will. You blame yourself for something, but somewhere in your mind, you know that everything happens with God's will. Scott and I saw our daughter in the incubator. She was so delicate. A nurse who was on duty guided us; we had to be very careful as there were several tubes attached to her body. When I asked the nurse, "What can I do for my baby?" I was full of emotions that a newborn's mother goes through. I wanted to hold my baby, but I couldn't, and this was causing so much anguish inside me, which led me to ask this question from the nurse. Luckily, the nurse was very sensible and trained. She told me, "You can feed the baby, but not directly latching her to your breast." I felt a little wave of happiness inside my heart. I could not be thankful to God enough for letting my baby and me at least go this far.

The nurse explained to me further that they feed such premature babies in a different manner. They collect the mother's breast milk and dip a cloth-type material to drop or dab the cloth on the baby's lips. My heart skipped a beat, and I was amazed at God's ways of caring for every living being on this earth. It was surprising for me to know that despite being in the incubator, my daughter would still be getting some drops of her mother's breast milk. She will know the smell of her mother's milk. I was told once by the nurses that babies recognise the voice of their mothers. I had this in my mind, and through a small hole in the incubator, I started talking to my daughter. I broke down into tears. My husband grabbed me from my shoulders and whispered in my ear, "Our daughter can feel your emotions, so if we stay strong, she will be strong and will fight through it. But we have to be patient and hold our emotions." He then continued, "If you are going to be upset, our daughter will be upset as well." I said to my daughter, "Whatever it is, we will be with you the whole way." I just sat there singing for her slowly and giving my milk to be fed to my daughter. In order to feed her, I had to give the milk in a syringe. The nurse dipped a cloth in it and then dabbed it on my daughter's lips. It was hard to see my daughter lying like a tiny little angel in the incubator. Several tests were being done daily to monitor how she was doing. Undoubtedly, the hospital was fantastic, and we couldn't have asked for better care than the nurses and other staff here provided.

When I reached home in the evening, I was desperately waiting for my mother to be home. Being the only daughter, we were very close to each other. After going through all this trauma, all I wanted was my Mum. She was my go-to person for every battle I had fought in my life. The moment she reached home, I just launched on her with a big hug and broke into tears in her arms. She started crying with me. I said, "You know, Mum, I have given birth to a baby. Can you believe it?" She comforted me and asked me not to worry, "Just pray, and everything will be alright. Most of the babies born early make it through." I told her, "Whatever it is, nothing is in my control. I can just cry, blame myself, and wonder where I went wrong. All the nurses told me that it could happen to anybody. They told me this placenta abruption could happen to anybody, regardless of their physique or health conditions. The only thing that I can do is be there for my daughter."

On the seventh day, the doctors tried to put her off of the ventilator by putting her on a high-flow machine. This type of machine supports the baby; however, it is not a ventilator. They tried to explain everything to us before shifting her to the other machine. The doctors wanted to see how our daughter responds to it. It is like the baby leads the way forward. So, our daughter was on a high fluency machine on the 7th day, but after 24 hours, she started to struggle. The doctors explained earlier that some babies might not respond well, and we will have to decide if she needs to go back on the ventilator. They also performed a blood test to tell the correct picture of why she was struggling to breathe. The readings from the test were not very good. They told us that she needed extra support and that some babies struggle and come out of it; however, some babies don't. So, I said, "Okay, if this is required, I will go for it." She was put back on a ventilator, and her heartbeat was restored.

Chapter 7
The Dark Days

I kept away from my friends and family all this time, as there was nothing that I wanted except for my daughter to get well. I was in no frame of mind to talk to anybody apart from the ones who were very close to me, my Mum and Dad, and my God. I was not even in contact with my best friends. The last thing I wanted at this time was people questioning what had happened. Or dealing with queries like 'Why was my baby born early?' I was not ready to answer any such questions. There were already millions of questions going on inside me. I had enough on my plate to deal with. I did not have the energy to cater to other people's curiosity. The days were passing by, and finally, on the 13th day, I was able to hold my daughter in my arms for the first time. It was an absolutely magical experience. The long wait to hold her was finally over. Until that day, I didn't even know if I would ever be able to hold her. That day, the nurses on duty asked me if I wanted to hold my baby. I was shocked and asked, "Really, can I hold my baby?" I couldn't believe my ears. She said, "Yes, you can. Although it's not going to be easy, we can make it happen." She was on a ventilator with so many tubes running in and out of her.

The feeling at that time when I held her with all the tubes was so precious. I could not hold the gushing tears mixed with the feeling of joy. It seemed that my greatest wish had been answered. I could never forget that moment in my life. When I looked at her, I had a wave of thought that angels do exist. She seemed to be nothing less than a precious God-sent angel in our life.

My daughter was sleeping most of the time as she was on morphine. The doctor said that they had to keep her on morphine as the ventilator was not very comfortable. I was also in a lot of pain from the epidural injections that were given to me every day. This pain remained for quite a significant amount of time. The side effect of the injection was the spearing pain, not like a migraine but as if I were being stabbed in the head with a knife. However, I did not lose my patience, and my hope increased my endurance. Although I felt as if my head would fall off, holding my daughter in my arms was above anything in the world, beyond any pain. I held her in my arms for 3 to 4 hours; it was a heavenly experience. My husband could not hold her as she was very small, but he was sitting next to me and kept saying he was fine as long as I got to hold her. We took pictures with our daughter, talked to her, and said, "Oh my God, you're in my arms, baby girl." My husband video called my Mum so she could see our daughter, and my Mum started talking to her. She told my daughter, "I am your grandma, and I love you so much." It was such a difficult and emotional phase of my life. Due to COVID, nobody else was allowed to visit the hospital besides for any serious illnesses, so she couldn't visit us.

Every day, my husband and I went back and forth between the hospital and home to see our daughter. The feeling of each day going to the hospital was scary and daunting, not knowing what the doctors were going to say or what tests they would want to conduct. Each day was a struggle for us, but Mum kept me strong by saying, "I'm praying. I have kept this fast and prayed a specific prayer. Our princess (as she always called our daughter by this name) will be fine." I struggled in the hospital emotionally, breaking at times. I also remember seeing a few other parents going the same way, crying inside the parents' room, just breaking down and losing patience.

My mother was working during those days from the office and had to go to work despite the coronavirus spreading. Later, her work became hybrid; she had to go to work every alternate day. Since my husband and I were going to the hospital regularly in hopes of seeing our little angel as any other normal child, our consultant suggested we take each day as it comes. She told us, "There might be surprises, some unexpected outcomes, and again, we will try to take your daughter off of the ventilator when we deem it to be appropriate."

During the short life of my newborn daughter, they tried to take her off of the ventilator at least five times, but her lungs could not cope up without it as was expected. She kept struggling, and her lungs could not stand the excessive amount of work they had to do in order to keep her breathing intact. During those two and a half months of our hospital visits to see our daughter, we could see her growing and responding with her eyes whenever I used to communicate with her. Today, when I look back, I feel that life itself is just like a game where nobody knows how long they are present in others' lives and unaware of how long they are part of this world. Your game is over once you breathe your last breath. Now I have a very clear picture of life where I see it as nothing but a small bubble. Everybody will perish as every bubble either vanishes into thin air or mixes in moisture.

All you can do is cry after losing your loved ones or, for that matter, any person; you can't stop living yourself. My mind has come to accept the fact that life still goes on, even after losing a person who means the world to you. It is the norm of this whole universe. One's death does not stop the world from moving. Everyone else keeps living, and eventually, people move on in their life. However, few losses leave a deep hollow void inside you, which I never knew until I was actually hit by this harsh reality.

I had my hopes high that my little baby would soon be alright. My mother gave me a lot of courage and built my faith strong that my daughter would soon be among us. I still remember that it was my mom's birthday, the 13th of September, 2020. We were all sitting together for breakfast, and my mom tried to lighten up the mood by reminding us about Nando's. My mother loved Nando's. Upon my mother's remarks about it, I bluntly said, "Mom, I am completely not in that frame of mind."

My mother comforted me by saying, "Everything is in God's hand. You need not worry and deal with every day as it unfolds."

Chapter 8
A Double Tragedy

It is hard to live a life where you see everything falling apart one by one. Though it was sudden, it seemed that my tragedies were like a domino effect. The year 2020 was the toughest one to live and survive with what my life had served me.

After all the trials to remove my precious little angel off the ventilator with no success, we were back to the same place where my daughter was breathing with support. The worst part was that we had no clue for how long. Our days were spent visiting the hospital and spending time with our daughter. Every time I came close to my daughter and looked into her angel eyes, I used to tell her that she would come out of this and we would fight through it soon. It was already hard for me to cope with the stress of post-delivery, and, every day, looking at my daughter going through the pain of being on the ventilator was hurtful on its own. It was getting hard for me to maintain my brain's normal working level. At that time, there was a lot that was going on inside my mind. However, my mom kept comforting me with her sweet, positive words of hope and encouragement. She was my only go-to person and the strongest anchor in my deepest sorrows.

The days were still passing by with all my fears and anxiety for the unknown future. I still remember very well it was a Tuesday of the 9th of October, 2020, when my Mum told me that she was feeling very weak. She had a number of health problems and lived with them for years. Though my mother was obese and lived with a number of pains, she was a soldier for me, fighting many battles with honour and grace. No matter what, every day, she used to get up even in pain, pop a painkiller, and start her day. Never did she ever complain. However, my Mum had multiple underlying problems already - high blood pressure, diabetes, arthritis, knee issues, and her body wore her down quite a lot. She struggled to lose the weight even when she tried, as I found out later on in her good diary that she wrote in - bless her. It hurts me to think that if only this worked, things would have been different right now. That day, when she told me that she was not feeling good and felt too weak, it raised my ears. I was already very concerned about my parents since March 2020, when the whole world was hit by the coronavirus pandemic.

We had just celebrated Mum and Dad's 35th anniversary in February 2020. That was their last anniversary that we celebrated. Who knew? Mum arrived in the UK when she was 18 years old and took over a huge responsibility. Mum left her family behind in India and performed many roles; a wife and a daughter-in-law (taking care of the in-laws). She fulfilled her roles beautifully throughout. Despite the ups and downs that came her way, Mum continued fulfilling her responsibilities.

I kept telling my parents that they needed to be careful as it was not only about us; we needed to be cautious for the unborn child as well. On 9th October 2020, I talked to my husband and told him that Mum was not feeling good, and she kept saying that she was feeling weak. I did not even go to see my daughter that day since I had a lot of pain due to my epidural and the events that followed during the day. My husband told me to take a break and stay home, and he would go alone to see our daughter. He knew what I had been going through since delivering my daughter; the pain of epidural, the post-delivery hospital stays, and seeing my daughter on the ventilator all took a great toll on my physical well-being. I resisted a little staying at home and not being able to see my daughter, but then I thought that my health was also very important. If I were unwell myself, I couldn't be there for my daughter, who needed my care the most. I booked a physiotherapist to come home and give me a massage that might lessen my epidural pain a little.

My Mum still cooked that afternoon and went to take a nap, telling me that she was not feeling right. Since my childhood, I have seen my mother as the strongest, most resilient, and remarkable woman. With her always beside me, I never felt much need to have any friends. The way she took care of her family was exemplary, and I do not see myself anywhere close to the level where she stood in caring, vigilant about our needs, and steadfast in helping and providing everything that I wanted throughout my life. The level of strength that she had made all of us worried this time since we never saw her complaining that she wasn't feeling well. This time, it seemed to be very different. She was my rock, and now, looking at her lying on the bed sleeping was a very uncomfortable feeling. One might say, generally, children do not like their mothers resting for a while, but I was getting very different vibes looking at her in this state. I was her only daughter and the closest person to her. I was not over the pain that I felt seeing my daughter each passing day, and now my heart was sinking for my mother.

When my husband came back from the hospital, I told him once again that Mum was not feeling well. He became a little worried now. Initially, my husband took my mother's sickness as a normal viral fever, but he got concerned when I told him the same upon his return. Until the end of that day, we did not notice any further progression in my mother's illness. However, on Wednesday, 10th of October 2020, I woke up hearing my mother talking to the doctor, who advised her to go for a COVID test. My parents talked to me, and my father told me that my mother would have to go for the drive-thru COVID test. So, I made an appointment for her, and my father took her there the same day for her COVID test. I also talked to the hospital where my daughter was admitted, and to my horror, they told us not to visit my daughter until my mother's COVID test results came out. I completely ran into panic, wondering what was going on with me. I said to myself, "This can't be happening." We had to self-isolate.

By this time, my mother had already come back from the drive-thru COVID test. She was not feeling well and kept sleeping in her room upstairs. My parents were upstairs while we were downstairs using separate toilets, self-isolating from each other. We told my mother and father that they must stay upstairs while we would remain downstairs and whatever they needed, we assured them that we would provide them with everything upstairs. There were two toilets, and we could use one exclusively for ourselves. We could not afford to have COVID at this stage, and we were rightly staying apart from Mum and Dad until we got the result since we were not sure whether my mother was COVID-positive. At the same time, we were trying to find out if there was any way we could get the results earlier because the delay meant that we could not see our daughter in the hospital. We kept on finding out ways of getting my mother's results anytime earlier than expected. I was getting filled up with anxiety and longing to see my daughter. However, the hospital facility was amazingly helpful; they kept on sending us videos and photos of my daughter.

At least I could have a look at her. Of course, I could not resist my feelings of not being able to see my daughter in person, and whenever I saw the pictures, I would break down into tears. It was already so difficult for me to leave my daughter in the hospital, and now I could not even go and see her. It was like I had left a piece of my heart in the hospital.

This motherly feeling was totally unknown until my daughter was born. I could have never speculated this worry and anxiety beforehand. Life certainly changes after you become a mother. My daughter's birth made me a completely different person. Today, I can not bear the pain of not having a single sight of my daughter and being there with her. If I come to think about it, it was just a few months back that I was living my life without her.

"Being a mother is learning about strengths that you did not know you had and dealing with fears that you did not know existed."

- Linda Wooter

Chapter 9
The Self-isolation Days

For me, my Dad, and my husband, it was a difficult chapter altogether, facing the double tragedy. My mother fell sick, and all of us were in self-isolation, waiting for the reports to come and ward off our anxieties. My Mum was in her room upstairs, where I kept a constant check asking her on video calls if she was okay and if she wanted anything to eat.

Panning from outside, our house had a cute and small landscape with a small driveway. My parents were extremely fond of gardening due to their love of nature and green living, often eating organic food. There was a small garden at the backside of our house, with a small wooden breakfast area connecting to the lower portion of the backyard. It was a two-storey house with connecting stairs in the hall leading upstairs, where my parents were isolating in their room. Although there were two more rooms upstairs, we preferred staying in the room in the lower portion that had an attached bath, which was normally used as a guest room. We could not afford to take the risk of getting positive ourselves at this time. Since the kitchen is downstairs, I took over the charge of preparing and delivering the food upstairs to my parents.

All the time, I was worried, not only for my daughter but also for my mother's deteriorating condition each day. I could see her on the video call, how weak she was feeling. She would repeatedly refuse to eat by saying that she did not feel like eating since she was not feeling good. However, we kept doing whatever we could to get the food to my parents upstairs and at least make them eat something even if they did not feel like it. She was a resilient lady and never complained of her sickness. As far as I remember, none of us ever had to experience her prolonged sickness. She had strong willpower and kept herself on her toes even if she was not feeling well, to serve her family in the best ways possible without failing. This time it was all very odd and new to us.

I had lots of things going on in my mind at that time. Somewhere inside my heart, I kept praying for my mother to get a negative result on her COVID PCR test. However, unfortunately, my utmost fear, my Mum's COVID result came out positive. So the days passed, and we kept dealing with our worries. We continued anticipating how and when all of this would be over.

In the middle of the 11th and 12th of October's night (almost the 12th morning), I heard my father shouting for me to get the oximeter since my Mum could not breathe easily. My heart was pounding with fear as I had woken up to my father's shouting. My husband rushed to get the oximeter, and both of us entered my parents' room with our masks and gloves on. I saw my Mum lying on the bed. She could hardly talk because of her bad condition. She could just say, "I don't feel good."

It was all very unreal, whatever was happening right in front of my eyes. I heard the doctor saying that my Mum's condition was critical then and that we must shift her to the hospital or must call the ambulance. We checked her oxygen level at that time; it was extremely low at 55. My senses seemed to be frozen, and I could not comprehend if this was actually happening with my Mum. I kept wondering how I could help her to make her feel okay. We felt completely clueless about what was going on as it was something we had never experienced before.

We called the ambulance and waited for it to reach our place. I was looking at my Mum and at the same time had my daughter in my mind, without any idea what was actually happening with my family. My thoughts were moving randomly as I was totally clueless. The ambulance took almost an hour to come; the crew went in to get my Mum. It was completely morning by then. The crew was talking to my Mum, and they had already put her on oxygen. I remember asking my Mum if she were okay. I kept telling her that she was going to be okay as I was standing at the bottom of the stairs while they were bringing her down. The crew asked my Mum if she wanted to lie down, and they brought her down on the stretcher? She refused right away and told them that she would walk down the stairs of the house. Who knew that this would be the last time she would be walking in the house? None of us knew that my Mum going to the hospital from the house was actually her farewell to her final abode.

While she walked down the stairs and reached the final step where I was standing, I still don’t know what struck me at that time that I grabbed her hand and told her, “Mum, everything is going to be okay!” My Mum was leaving the house for the last time. Her footsteps were moving outside towards the ambulance, and I was standing, looking at her from behind. Thankfully the CCTV installed outside our house captured her last footsteps going out of the house, approaching the ambulance parked on our driveway.

She was a strong woman with the willpower of iron or steel. It was unbelievable that somebody in that condition still preferred to walk outside up to the ambulance instead of being carried on a stretcher. I can say with confidence that such people are rare to find these days. She was 54, and I remember looking at her walking and standing for the last time in her life. The memories are so fresh still and perhaps can never fade even to the slightest level. My husband was quickly bagging her stuff; her bag, toilet seat, and charger, putting them inside the ambulance for her.

"Mum, if I could have one last chance to meet you, I would just ask you to hug me as tight as you can. I miss you a lot!"

I was still not over my daughter's critical condition, and now I was thrown into the pain of watching my mother getting hospitalised as well. I watched her leave our house for the hospital, but my hopes never left my side. I truly believed that everything would be okay and the whole family would be together, along with my newborn daughter.

Mum and I shared a very special mother-daughter bond. I could share all my worries and anxieties with my whole and the only soulmate around - MUM. If it was somebody else at my place (God forbid), they would have fought the same fears for their mother with some critical illness. I felt very heartbroken inside seeing all that was happening. But I could not show it on my face because of my father and even my mother, who remained strong even while going down the stairs and leaving for the hospital in the ambulance. I had to pull myself up and present myself strong enough at least to pass on the good vibes in trying to bring back the sparkle on my father's and Mum's face. I guess I must admit now that I failed big time in doing it at that time. I tried my best to toil up this rough patch that we were going through. My senses took a couple of minutes to comprehend the intense trauma and agony of myself and my whole family. However, there was nothing to very little that we could have done to reduce the aftermath of this turmoil.

"You never know how strong you are until being strong is the only choice you have."

-Bob Marley

Chapter 10
A Difficult Farewell

It was the most challenging time of my life when I had to let my Mum go alone to the hospital, without even knowing what the future held for her. While she was going, all of us thought that she would be gone for a few days and come back. However, God had his own plans. We still had to self-isolate and get the house sterilised with the disinfectant spray. Even after the ambulance and the paramedic staff came, Mum had to wait for good 30-40 minutes due to some checks and balances. After she left, all three of us were in deep thoughts about what had just struck us.

Since my daughter's birth, I just wanted somebody to console me all the time and share all my fears with me. Having my Mum with me, I never needed anybody else to share my griefs and sorrows. But, that day, I was feeling lonely and stranded after my Mum left for the hospital. My worries doubled, and my anxiety increased two-fold. First, the separation from my daughter, then my mother. I was not used to being on my own and dealing with everything happening in my life. I had never faced tough times like these before, as far as my memory carried me back in my childhood.

As mentioned earlier, Mum went to the hospital on the 12th of October, 2020, due to an extremely low oxygen saturation level. She remained on a video call with us while she was going to the hospital and even after she reached there. She told us, "Don't worry, I'm waiting to be transferred to one of the wards." In the hospital, before taking her to the ward, she was asked to wait in the lobby for quite a long time, where she turned quite frustrated. Since none of us could accompany her to be admitted to the isolation ward, all of us were in great worry. We had no idea what was going on, and as Mum was on her own, she became restless, worried, and started panicking.

It was such a difficult time for her and us, as no one could be with her. I told her to let me find out what was happening by calling Eligible Medical Expenses (health insurance). I called them up and told them, "My mother is there at your hospital, and she's been waiting for so many hours. She is unwell and getting too frustrated. Can you tell us what's going on?" The person on the other side of the line replied, "We have just been really busy and are very occupied at the moment. We will have to see how and where we can shift her after the doctors check her, and soon, we will shift your Mum to the ward." At this point, I thought that this was the worst situation since no one could be with her.

Simultaneously, I was coordinating with my daughter's

hospital as well; my husband made sure that he was helping in the best way he could. The hospital staff told us, “Your daughter is still the same and on the ventilator.” I asked the hospital to make some personal arrangements so we could keep track of our daughter and see her; otherwise, I would not be able to cope. I told them that they would have to make arrangements since we had to isolate for another 15 days, which was very hard for me. The hospital made an arrangement with the nurses and the staff for us to see our daughter on the video call three times a day. The nurses were just like a family to my daughter when we could not be there, as the hospital was her home. She was so loved and so well looked after. She was in her own little cubicle, and the nurses kept sending us photos and took our photos with me as well. At least it kept us going.

In the meanwhile, my Mum was shifted to the normal COVID ward, where we could do a conference video call with her and Dad. She was still complaining about not feeling good and was also frustrated to be in the hospital. She said, “I do not like being here,” and neither did she like the food that was being given to her there. During the video call, my husband often asked for the monitor readings on the instruments around her, like oxygen level, heart rate, and pulse rate. On the other hand, at home, my Dad was still isolating himself in the room upstairs while we were downstairs, providing everything to him at the room's door.

Then, my husband started having severe body aches. He would just lie on the floor in the living room, complaining about not feeling too good. All during this time, I kept thinking, why was God punishing us? I tried not to think much about Mum being at the hospital; I was worried that she had COVID, but I prayed that she would come back home soon.

The very first day when she was hospitalised, she was joking and laughing with us. I still had faith that she would soon be home and come back to her normal self. On the first and second days, it was pretty normal. However, after that, my Mum started getting really tired and was already homesick. She was also messaging her friends in response to their messages asking about her welfare, telling them, "I will be home in just a few days."

The most difficult part for her started when she was put on oxygen support, and she had to wear a very tight mask. We kept calling my Mum in the hospital and would regularly take updates from the nurses on her progress along with talking to Mum about how she actually felt. Upon talking to the nurses, I was told that Mum had to wear the mask to obtain oxygen for at least 10 hours a day. She was struggling to keep the mask on as it was too painful. She was complaining about how much discomfort it was to wear that mask since it was of a different kind. She would wear it only for a few hours, and she used to say things like she would die wearing it; it was that uncomfortable. To this, I would tell my Mum, "This is what will make you better, so you have to wear it, bearing the discomfort attached to it. Mum, please listen to me."

The days kept going, with us taking updates from both the hospitals, i.e., where my Mum and daughter were. During this time, it seemed that my Mum would come back once the oxygen level got back to normal.

We kept a regular check on my Mum; however, we could see that her health was deteriorating. One day, when my husband, my Dad, and I were on a video call with her, I saw the doctor and knew instantly that this couldn't be good. I didn't want to hear anything or hear the word deteriorating, but this was true. My Mum told us that she wasn't getting better. We called the hospital and talked to the concerned doctor. The doctor told us that it would be like giving us false hope if he said that my Mum had more than a 30% chance of survival. I could not believe what the doctor was saying and denied it completely, saying, "You do not know my Mum. She is very strong and has lived in lots of pain so gracefully for a number of years. She can do this." He said that he had been a doctor with 30 years of experience in the same ICU ward, and he would rather be realistic by saying that there was only a 30% chance of my Mum's recovery. My father and husband consoled me by saying, "Your Mum is very strong; we all will pray, and she will make it."

At the same time, after my Mum left for the hospital and my husband started having severe body aches, we ordered our COVID test kits, which we received the next day. We were already in self-isolation, and there were only a few days left till it would be over. However, after receiving the kits, we had to send out the samples by posting at a certain post box. We were still self-isolating and waiting until the results came out. On the 19th of October, 2020, results came out, and all three of us were tested positive for COVID. This meant that we had to go further into isolation which made me scared and extremely worried. After sharing the results on our family group, Mum became more worried too. She had already been crying for the past two days, saying that she was tired of staying at the hospital. I thank my senses today that I took photos and screenshots of both my daughter and Mum during our video calls.

I sent our daughter's pictures that the hospital had sent on our family group and those that I took during the video call (which the hospital management very kindly facilitated us with) when the nurses would show our daughter. To almost all of the pictures, my Mum's remarks would be, “I want to hold you,” “I hope you get better,” “My princess,” “I miss you,” or “I want to hold you.” This was as close as we all could get to being together as a family. As much as I wanted to see my daughter in my Mum's arms, by this time, my hopes had taken a different turn as I was now thinking and praying for my Mum to come home.

Meanwhile, my husband had severe body temperature, and his body was aching to the level where he felt it was being crushed; it was that bad. However, we were doing our own home remedies that I got to know from my father-in-law in India, like the use of turmeric, putting black seed oil in our nose, and some herbal ayurvedic medicine known to treat coronavirus that my brother-in-law sent from India. When we called our daughter's hospital, the doctor told us that before coming to the ward, we must make sure that we were completely free from the virus and tested negative. Of course, they wanted to ensure the safety of other patients and the medical staff, as we could be the carriers and put others' lives in danger. I had come to terms with the circumstances and remained calm, in spite of the fact that I could not see my daughter up close and personal.

On the same day (19th of October, 2020), when the three of us tested positive, we could see my Mum on the video call wearing a long tight yellow mask. Her nose was sore, and she had trouble breathing. She looked too tired, perhaps from the struggle to keep breathing. I felt that her health was deteriorating, to my utter disbelief. We spoke to the doctors and nurses to enquire how she was doing. They told us, "She still requires a lot of oxygen. We might have to put her on the ventilator; the oxygen level is still going very low. She is not improving; instead, her condition is deteriorating." The three of us started to think about what this meant. Since we all had tested positive, we were isolating within our own residence and only came out of the room when we had to discuss something or needed support from each other during this stressful time. I still had positive thoughts for my Mum that she'd come out of this, even if she were to be put on the ventilator. Somewhere, in the back of my mind, I kept thinking of how when my grandfather went on the ventilator and was in a critical condition for 48 hours, he made it through. Therefore, I wanted to keep my hopes high for my Mum that she would come out of the ventilator once her oxygen level got to normal.

The doctors and nurses kept in touch with us as my mom was unable to pick up her own phone due to her condition. On the Zoom video call, doctors showed us my Mum, who was still struggling to breathe. The doctors told us that her oxygen level was going very low, which was why she needed to be put on ventilator support. I was crying all the time looking at her. I knew she was very tired and could not talk. I told her, "Mum, you can fight through this. You are very strong." She just expressed with her hand gesture, telling us that 'she might be going.' I could not believe my fate that after my daughter, I had to see my mother on the ventilator as well. My Mum was talking to my father, but she could not speak much. While I was crying, my husband and father told me that we would pray for her and soon come out of this. I recorded everything on our Zoom video call, but unfortunately, the sound was not recorded. My Mum's gestures and expressions that day (20th October 2020) made my heart sink, and my whole body became really weak. I never knew that I would have to go through the pain I was never prepared for and had no strength inside. However, I still remained positive that this was just a phase our family was going through, and everything would be settled when my Mum came back home. Doctors told us that she would require 80-90% oxygen. We had no choice but to accept putting her on the ventilator. We were given the number of her ward to call and know how she was doing.

I remember I used to call day and night, where they had the same answer that there was no sign of improvement. After putting my Mum on the ventilator on the 21st of October 2020, the only thing that the doctors and nurses had in their defence was to probe the patient. However, it did not help much. Her stats were the same; she required 100% oxygen even after eight hours. While on a video call with my daughter, I would go and cry in the corner. While talking to Mum, I would tell her, "Come on, Mum, get up. Your princess is waiting for you."

I was on a Zoom video call with her. As the nurses held the camera in front of her, I remember very well that it was so painful to see her lying so helpless and totally unconscious. I broke into tears looking at her and said, "Mom, I have cooked *chapatti* for you. Please wake up! Please wake up!"

She was just lying there still, but I knew she could hear me. I told her, "Mom, I know you are strong. Just give your best."

In spite of the fact that my mother was just 54 and a woman with strong willpower, looking at her like that made me realise that it is very important we take care of our internal health and physical well-being. Negligence towards our health can take a great toll when someone actually falls sick. Though she was strong, her internal complications prevented her from showing any improvement.

When we tested positive, I was heartbroken again because it meant that we would not be able to see our daughter for another 15 days. After I called my daughter's ward and informed them about the whole situation, they told us that if we went to see my Mum, we would have to isolate ourselves for another 15 days. I had already not seen my daughter for about 21 days, and now further isolation/separation was about to hit my face. We had not left the house, we had not seen our daughter, and we had not been able to go to the hospital where my Mum was. The doctors kept telling us that there was no improvement in Mum and we needed to prepare for the worst. She was still requiring 90% oxygen. However, finally, I found relief when I got to see my daughter on the 25th of October, 2020. I made a Zoom call to my mother from the hospital and showed my daughter in the video, telling her,

"Please get better for your granddaughter. She wants to see you in better health."

My mother breathed her last breath on the 30th of October, 2020. I still remember that day; we were going to drop my father off at the hospital so that he could see my Mum. I could not see her myself because otherwise, I would not have been able to visit my daughter in the hospital. I had already been separated from her for over 20 days. It was a tough choice to make. It was a test by God where I was stuck choosing between the two most beloved people in my life. While I was locking the door to drop my father off at the hospital, I received a call from the doctors, informing us that Mum's condition was worsening rapidly and it might be the time. I told them that we were on our way and before I could even realise what had just hit me and recollect my senses, I received another call from the hospital while we were still driving. They informed us that she was gone!

Although the doctors told us beforehand that Mum was not going to make it, we were still not prepared. I was totally dumbfounded when I heard the doctor telling me that Mum was no more. It was like the floor was swept away from my feet. The difference between receiving the first call and the last one telling us that she was no more was about 5 minutes. We could not manage to reach the hospital to drop Dad off in time, to be there with Mum breathing her last breath. Finally, we reached and dropped Dad off, but I could not enter the premises because of my daughter, for whom I had to complete the isolation period. Dad sat with Mum for a few hours after she was gone. I went to see my daughter, but my brain was not working. I was holding my daughter, trying to be strong, but it seemed somehow impossible at that time. I was too shattered to hold myself.

Chapter 11
The Positive Side of the Story

"Now I know why you always told me to be strong, you knew that one day I would need the strength to bear your loss."

-Anonymous

No matter how old you are, the loss of a mother changes your life forever. Your mother is your first love and forever friend, and for me, it was no different. I can never really get over the loss of my Mum. However, with the passage of time, I have learnt to live without her. I feel the loss every moment of my day, but I never lose the courage to pick up myself and move on.

As I mentioned earlier, we could not manage to reach the hospital to drop Dad off in time to be there with Mum breathing her last breath. And when we did reach there and dropped Dad off, I could not enter the premises because of my daughter, for whom I had to complete the isolation period. While I was dropping my father at the hospital, I did not want to come out of there at all. It was like I wanted myself to be swallowed by the earth so I didn't have to move ahead or backwards. My husband came out of the car and told me that we had to go to our daughter as we were getting late. Dad sat with Mum for a few hours after she had left this world. Although I went to see my daughter, my brain was just numb. I was holding my daughter and did my best to be strong, but it just seemed impossible at that time. I was too shattered to hold myself.

My Mum lived a beautiful life and passed away at the age of 54. She would always tell the nurse that I would go soon because she had been suffering from lots of pains and aches. After seeing our daughter, we picked up Dad from the hospital and went home. I could not believe what was going on, and I couldn't accept the fact that my Mum was gone. I was constantly crying in the car, and my husband supported me and told me that even though she was gone, I needed to be strong for the rest of the family.

Sometimes life throws you into situations where you are left with nothing but to make a choice between something that you dread in your life. I had to make the toughest choice of my life when I had to decide between seeing my mother for the last time and staying close to my daughter, who was already on the ventilator. I wanted to go and sit with my Mum, at least during her final farewell. While I was with my daughter crying, I told her, "Look, your *nanni* is gone."

We had to ring and inform the family, priests, and friends. In the last few days, I had received lots of calls from all acquaintances, each of them asking about my Mum’s condition. My reply was, “She does not look really good.” All of them gave me courage by saying things like, “Don't lose hope. Your Mum is very strong. She will be fine really soon.” I was not in good condition, but I had to inform everyone about my Mum passing away. I just uploaded it on my social media since it was easier to inform everybody that way. Somehow, I did not want to deal with everything. After reaching home, we had to do our prayers, which, in our culture, are performed every 13 days after a woman passes away. We had to light up the ghee candle, which is supposed to be lit constantly until the last thirteenth day. On the thirteenth day, the priest comes up to pray, and this is when we let the soul go away. We believe that until thirteen days, the soul is somewhere around us, and until then, a lot of care and precaution is taken to keep the candle lit.

The priest comes on, and that is when we cut all ties and let the soul go away. I was mentally and physically tired. My husband (may God bless him) and I slept next to the candle every night to make sure that it was lit all the time, for which we both had to sleep on the floor. Since I was going through the trauma and the aftermath of this massive loss of my soulmate, my husband made sure that he was constantly checking on the ghee candle. He knew that it would be very difficult for me to face this reality and took extra care in giving me his maximum support during that difficult time. The candle or the holy fire to monitor is called *'diya,'* and we have to be vigilant not to let it diminish.

We made sure that the candle remained lit and placed my Mum's photo next to her favourite plants that she had bought and kept on her couch. We also made a garland of fresh flowers to put on her picture for thirteen consecutive days. I was amazed at how God plans and how we are never aware of what those plans are. If my daughter had been born on the 27th of October according to the given due date, my mom would have never seen her at all. I was totally stuck choosing between having a chance to see my Mum during her last days versus completing my 21 days isolation period and holding my daughter. It was such a tough choice to make, but I had to see and be close to my child as I had already been away from her for the past few days. She was so small and tiny that my heart always skipped a beat upon having a glimpse of her. The day my mother passed away, I was heartbroken, and my grief was incomparable to any of the saddest events I had ever experienced. However, I regained my sanity back as I knew I was a mother too.

After the final prayer for the departed soul, I was still in disbelief that my Mum was gone and that too so soon. The pain that I was going through was an excruciating one. Our family was totally shattered with dissent and felt an enormous void that my mother left behind within us by passing away so soon.

Chapter 12
Another Goodbye

"There is something about losing a mother that is permanent and inexpressible - a wound that will never quite heal."

-Susan Wiggs

It seemed to me that overcoming the loss of my Mum was almost impossible. Our days of isolation and being affected by COVID were spent thinking about why our family was suddenly hit with so many losses. I could not register this terrible incident that had struck my soul so hard.

After completing our isolation period and testing negative for COVID, we finally got to see our daughter. Nurses and doctors had tried to remove her from the ventilator by putting a C-pep or a high-flow machine four or five times in the past. Our daughter would cross the 24 hours mark each time, but after that, she would struggle to breathe and would be put back on the ventilator. Being a premature baby and born without a heartbeat made it very difficult for her to breathe on her own. There are things that you might not know unless you are actually in a particular situation yourself. It was somewhat the same for us. I had no idea about this special ward for premature babies until I saw my baby lying in one. In the past two and a half months, we had seen parents coming into the ward for their children. They, too, went through the same struggle as I had. It was so surprising that a few months back, I didn't know such a ward existed. Nobody knows what their life might teach them in the future and how big of a test they might have to go through in that process. The two and half months of my daughter's life had been quite unpredictable for us as well; each time we put her off the ventilator, we did not know whether she would be able to make it. It was too much for the little soul. Every time we hoped that my child might make it, she ended up struggling.

It was tough for every parent visiting their newborn in that ward. Nobody spoke to each other as each parent struggled to see their little one in an incubator or on a ventilator. Few of the parents were of the view that *'We knew there wasn't something right.'* Then few would say, *'How did this happen as there was nothing that alarmed us before the delivery.'* We even came across mothers who gave birth to stillborns during that time, which was even more painful.

Due to the pandemic, it was challenging for us to visit our daughter every day. But then again, even when we did visit her, we could only watch her as she struggled to breathe with so many tubes attached to her tiny body. So I would just sit with her and talk to God, "God, are you there? If you are there and listening, please tell me how can this happen to the children who have done nothing?"

When going through hard times, you tend to question every aspect of life. You question what you have been through and everything you have done in your life, but there are no right or wrong answers in the end. It's like whatever was destined has to become a part of your life.

My husband has been a rock, supporting me throughout; he stood right next to me in every moment. I have been blessed enough to have him beside me, my soulmate, who held me and lifted me whenever I stumbled. He not only supported and held me but did the same for my Dad also. We all held each other through this tough time.

Then, there came a time when doctors began telling us that being on the ventilator was not easy for an adult, let alone a child this small; that did not count as the quality of life. Once we came to terms with this fact, we asked them what our next action plan should be. The doctor advised that we should remove her from the ventilator and let her choose her path to walk on.

Thus, we decided to remove her from the ventilator on the 18th of November 2020. Nobody knew what would happen after that for sure, but the doctors made a point to tell us that her chances of survival afterwards were slim so that we could prepare ourselves mentally.

For that day, I bought a red t-shirt for myself with L and O written on it, and another for my baby girl with V and E written on it. Once she was off the ventilator, I held her in my arms while my husband and Dad sat beside me. Nobody knew what would happen, so I held her close to me; my fear of losing her was gradually taking over my senses. She was my angel, who, like a warrior, fought for two and a half months on the ventilator. I knew how hard it had been for her tiny body. As we sat there, a few nurses who took care of our daughter with great diligence and responsibility were also there with us. They knew my daughter more than myself as they were the ones who spent more time being around my brave little angel, so we were comfortable having them around. It was such a moment that I wanted it to last for as long as possible, but I could barely control my emotions.

We had decided to bathe our baby with the help of the nurses to sort out the tubes and wires attached to her. Giving her a bubble bath with my husband holding her head was another special moment captured within my heart. It was a moment of bonding with our daughter, and we want to cherish this short-lived moment for a lifetime. This was before the final removal of the ventilator.

That day, my Dad came to see our daughter for the first time. My Mum's 13 days final ritual prayers were going on at that time as well, which itself took quite a toll on our emotional well-being. We were still struggling to come to terms with my Mum's death, and now we had to take the difficult decision of putting our angel off the ventilator.

I still remember my Dad walking through the door and approaching my daughter. He stood there for a while, staring at her with affection. My Dad held her in his arms, although it was challenging with all the tubes and wires attached to her. He tried to hold her with the utmost care, and the love of a grandparent was evident through his eyes as he looked right at his granddaughter. It was quite a task to move and take her into our arms with all the tubes, but with nurses around, it turned out to be really easy, with them holding the extended tubes connecting her and the ventilator while we held our angel. Of course, we could not move around much; all we could do was hold and stare at her beautiful face. My husband and I sat around my father when he was holding her; it was so unbelievable and adorable at the same time. We had a snow globe cube with us that had my Mum's picture inside; this was our small attempt to have the feel of my Mum around us all the time. That one place where my Mum would have been was where a long-desired grandchild was. My Mum had longed for a grandchild for the past seven years of our marriage. She always wanted to be around children who would call her *nanni*; she was fond of any child she came across.

We spent precious time with our daughter and made lots of memories. During my pregnancy, I had also arranged for the cast of my baby to be taken after the birth. Things were different now, so I talked to the lady to rearrange everything, explaining the whole scenario to her. With the COVID situation and my daughter's bleak chances of survival, I requested her to come to the hospital. She replied that she would be happy if the hospital permitted us. I pleaded with the hospital staff and told them that she was happy to be there with a form stating her as COVID negative. I told the hospital that I needed that and wanted to cast my daughter's hands and feet. It means the world to me to this day, as I can hold them and get the feeling as if I am holding her hands and feet.

All the days leading up to the 18th of November 2020 were about making memories with our daughter. I would pray and sing songs for her and take lots of photos. We also consulted a company called 'Remember my baby' (for remembrance photography). My husband also took some remarkable pictures. He has got an eye for detail and captures the best moments through his camera. Before the 18th of November, we requested the nurses close to our daughter to come for the care. I did a special prayer for my little angel the night before that day. I did not know how the day would unfold, but I had decided to stay strong. My very best friend gave those unique milestone cards to us, on which my husband wrote, "Whatever it is going to be, it will be. You will always remain exceptional and precious to us, and we are proud of you."

18th was very nerve-wracking. My daughter and I wore matching t-shirts; we had the doctors, nurses, Dad, and husband all around us. Before taking her off the ventilator, we decided to put her on the high-flow machines. Although my daughter did not like it very much, we wanted to give her the best possible chance of survival. My husband and I were taking turns in holding her when she was on the high-flow machines. I remember we were approaching the evening time. The hospital staff was kind enough to prepare a room for us, which was a little away from the ward, but we told them that we would be fine staying beside our angel and watching her heartbeat reading and staying close to her. We decided to monitor her heartbeat, heart rate, and oxygen level ourselves. The doctors said that it is entirely the parents' discretion whether they want to stay there or in a separate room. We wanted to hold her and see the readings simultaneously, so the nurses set up single beds for us in that room. My father went home at around 9:00 pm that evening. I told him to have some food; however, none of us bothered to eat ourselves. All we wanted was to spend time with our daughter.

Although the anxiety and discomfort within our hearts had left us with no appetite for anything, the nurses made sure to take good care of us. I am still very thankful to the hospital staff and nurses who kept bringing tea and coffee along with the most delicious toast to feed us from time to time. We are very thankful to the hospitals' nurses and doctors for their love as they became just like our family, as we spent an ample amount of time with them. As a mother, I tried my best to do whatever I could for my daughter during that time. Sailing through the most challenging time of my life, I still wanted to give my child my milk. It was such a difficult task as I was very stressed, and when you are stressed, you hardly produce any milk to nurse the child. It is sort of a vicious circle, and I was stuck in that same situation. However, with the help of the nurses, I managed to do whatever I could. I felt, as a mother, this was the least I could give my child.

From the 18th till the 22nd of November, we spent a memorable and precious time with our daughter; we went home once to change our clothes. On the 21st of November, we spoke to the nurses about having a room that was just slightly off that ward because we had not slept for three days. The nurses acknowledged us immediately and prepared that room for us. My husband and I went to the room to freshen up. We said to ourselves, "We can sleep tonight in this room, and if something happens, they can ring us, or they already know where we are to inform us." We decided that we would have some rest or might as well take turns after to compensate for our sleep deprivation. I went outside the room to inform the nurse about us resting that night. While I was walking towards the nurse, I saw her coming in my direction. As the nurse and I met in the corridor, she asked me to get my husband and come to the ward quickly. She said that our daughter's stats were falling very fast. I ran back to my husband and told him to come and see our daughter. We rushed to the ward and saw that her oxygen level was close to 10. We just held her close to us, and the nurses told us that they would stand outside and give us some time alone. As we held her close, my husband spoke to her, "Please come back, don't go!"

After a little while, we witnessed a miracle. For the 10 minutes that her stats were dropping, we were prepared for the worst, but then, after what my husband said to her, her oxygen level quickly went back to 100%. The nurse came back after a while and asked if everything was okay. The staff and doctors were amazed to see her come back to 100% and marked this as the most precious moment for them. It was such a miracle and a moment to treasure that we took photos. We understood that day that she did not want us to leave her side. She did not want us to go to the other room, so we stayed with her; her stats were doing phenomenally well, and her oxygen level was at 95-96. Her heartbeat was good as well after she gave us a little shock.

Another room that was initially offered to us was right next to the ward. The nurses suggested that we move into that room and have a little crib for our daughter to create a bit homey environment. There was a kettle and a toaster, with mattresses for us to sleep on. From the 21st to the 22nd, we stayed in that room, hearing my daughter's tiny breaths that gave me the feeling of a home. From time to time, nurses would come in and check in on our daughter. I felt that I should have opted for this room from the start.

While my husband was taking a nap, I held my daughter on my lap, talking to her, "Oh my god, you are so beautiful, all this time, your face was covered by tubes, and I could not see your pretty angel face properly."

It was such a heavenly moment, and talking about that day takes me back into that timespan, and I can still feel the softness of that precious moment. In the meantime, the doctors came to have a meeting with us. They told us, "We don't know for how long your child can go on like this. Some children can go on for days, weeks, and even months."

The doctors suggested that a hospice would be a better place to go, called Saint Martin's house, for us to spend some quality time as a family. So, after giving it a thought, I said, why not. It was an even more ideal place of retreat to spend some time with our daughter since there is an open space and gardens.

***

While we were talking and planning for Saint Martin's house, my husband lay on the bed next to the window with our daughter on his chest. This was the first time our little angel saw the light since the day she was born. It was such a precious moment. When the doctors came in, my husband apologised and told them, “Please don't mind if I keep lying with my daughter here.” Hence, I sat on chairs with them while my husband listened from the other end of the room. Then, having a good laugh, we told them that they did so much for us; what could we do for them in return?

After several days, my husband revealed to me that while our daughter was lying on her father's chest, she touched his fingers with her thumb and was drawing wings with his hands for her. After the doctors left our room, we were getting ready and waiting for the people to come from Martin’s house into our building to talk and take us there. We had a good family time with a nurse coming in and out, keeping a check on my daughter. I was holding my little angel while my husband made a video call to my father-in-law. He, too, was overwhelmed and excited to see his granddaughter. It was such a special moment for all of us. My hopes were getting higher, and I wanted to capture every moment of togetherness within those few minutes. At times, there are a few days or moments that leave a significant impact on our lives. I think this was that moment that left me spellbound. Little did I know that after this, I would always regret not having any device to freeze the time where it is.

As I held her in my arms that afternoon, I noticed a slight change in her colour. After a few seconds, she stopped breathing. It was at that moment that she breathed her last breath. I checked again to see any signs of breathing while my heart squeezed inside, and my senses went haywire. I wanted to scream in pain but did not seem to have any energy left. I tried to regain my strength to call for my husband and told him, “She’s gone.” My husband hung up my father-in-law’s call, saying, “I will call you back; we think she is gone.” I was still holding her in my arms. I felt lucky to be able to be there for her in her last moments.

For this reason, I did not feel comfortable even when I had to go to the loo, go home to change our clothes, or check up on my Dad. As much as I was broken in this challenging moment, the blessing that I could retract from this whole event was that she left while I held her tight in my arms. I told my daughter, “Thank you for going while you were in your mom’s arms; you could have been in the crib.” Instead, the little angel went so peacefully that I still cannot comprehend. I was so thankful that I did not see her struggle or suffer in pain; instead, she left her body so peacefully.

We informed the doctors and nurses, who came in to confirm that she was no more. The nurses told us that they would bathe her, although I did not comprehend anything that was happening around since we had never experienced any such thing.

We bathed her and took the prints of her tiny little hands and feet. I was mentally prepared, and it was such an unusual moment; I captured all of it through the video taken by a nurse.

We dressed her into a gown that was kept in the other room. It was a beautiful dress with pink hearts on it. There were several clothes that the doctors and nurses told us to use as they were bought for us from the money given as donations by many other families to be used in the care of intensively ill children. My husband trimmed her nails and combed her hair. She was extremely loved by her dad, and he was extremely attached to her. It was quite a challenging and testing time for us. There was a prayer playing in the background. It was quite a moment taking us to the heights of spirituality, centrality, and emotions, connecting directly to our lord.

My husband said, "Do you know, when I was lying there as I looked outside the window and she was making wings with my hands, I saw something in the sky. You know that I do not imagine things. I do not believe in these things and do not think much about them. However, to my surprise, I saw a huge face in the sky. It was slightly covered and looked like mom's face, followed by a little white horse with wings. Then I saw Lord Ganesh (who is the remover of all obstacles). I knew at that time as I had never seen anything like that ever and told our daughter holding her hands that I know you are going."

I was so amazed and shocked to know that my Mum came herself to take her. As if saying, "Sweetie, your time is with me now. Let's go." I felt so blessed at that very moment. What else could be a more significant holy blessing than Lord Ganesh coming himself to take our daughter?

We called a priest for the final rituals. However, the priest told us that there was no need for any final prayers or rituals as she was just a baby with no sins. He told us that kids below nine years of age are not cremated or need any ritual ceremonies as they are free from sins. I updated my friends and family on one platform as I just wanted myself to be alone. However, thanks to all our family and friends who stood by us at the funeral ceremony performed for our little angel. I was very proud of my daughter, who gave us these lovely two and a half months with her, as she could have gone the day she was born without a heartbeat. Nobody could take this feeling from us, being the proud parents that we were. We felt so proud to be this little angel's parents who gave us such beautiful memories; the love, the photos, and most importantly, knowing about her that she was a fighter. Also, I am so glad that my mom knew that she became a grandmother before she passed away. She bought her things and asked me about her granddaughter's health every time we used to talk on video call.

We wanted to arrange the best funeral for our daughter, just as we gave our mom a queen's send-off. We wanted to give her a princess send-off. We took her in a beautiful carriage with horses. It was pretty impressive, and we could also sit with her in that carriage. We arranged her funeral on the 17th of December 2020, and she expired on the 22nd of November 2020. There was a delay in the funeral due to the COVID outspread in our town. Therefore, it was hard to arrange the funeral ceremony before 17th December. We chose an amazingly scenic place for the burial of our daughter. The drive was fantastic, with birds chirping around the cemetery and lots of beautiful views all around it. Our daughter knew that her mom loved scenic beauty, and she went away that early to choose that place and lie peacefully there.

The funeral day was tough for all of us. Of course, no parents want to bring their child home in a box. We sat down beside her box and prayed. It was very emotional yet so spiritual. We took her in the carriage of horses, with us sitting and me singing and talking to her on the way to the final funeral. We led the whole ride with our friends and family following us.

I received another surprise that day, which was a big sign for what we named our daughter. The night before, I got several messages from my cousins, and one of my cousins wrote a lovely message stating our daughter's name. The message said,

"Although we didn't get to meet you, your name means colours. Tomorrow, please show your colours, and fill the skies with your beautiful hue."

So, we let off seven symbols that carry the soul to the final abode. On the day of the funeral, it was not even raining; my best friend came to me, tapped on my shoulder, and said, "Look at the sky!"

I went in complete shock when I saw a rainbow. She gave us a sign. It was so beautiful that we captured pictures of it, preserving it for our whole life to cherish this lovely scene through the eye of the camera lens, which left impressions on our hearts.

"When the links of life are broken and a child has to part, there is nothing that will ever heal a parent's broken heart."

Chapter 13
A Life of Love and Loss

Upon the loss of a loved one, grieving is a lifelong process. Even the deepest of physical wounds heal over time, but they leave a scar that acts as a constant reminder of the pain we endured. However, the death of a loved one is like a wound that never heals. It seeps blood till the day we leave this world to unite with our loved ones in Heaven, hopefully.

The deaths of my mother and daughter left me in immense grief. The fact that I lost them within days of each other had a huge impact on me. My heart ached to be able to hold my baby in my arms just one more time. But I couldn't do anything to soothe my aching heart, for my daughter lay in her casket buried deep under the soil. As pure and innocent as she was, her soul returned to Heaven. I crave to meet my Mum and daughter in heaven again.

My world seemed like a different place without Mum and my baby. There was a void, not just in my heart but also in my life. Now that Mum had left, I didn't know whom to turn to, and life without my baby seemed meaningless. I had so many dreams and aspirations for her, but all of them were washed away by a simple phenomenon called death. Death is like a predator that devours its prey in its entirety. All that is left behind are memories. I cherish the memories of all the times I spent with my Mum.

The two and a half months that I was privileged to spend with my daughter were perhaps the best times of my life. And yet, ironically, they were the worst times of my life too. Watching my baby die was not easy. It was as though someone was ripping off a part of me. I could not endure the sight of her; so weak and fragile, with tubes and catheters attached to her body. Yet she was the coolness of my eyes. I used to look at her for hours on end and not get bored. Her tiny features mesmerised me; I loved holding her little fingers and hands. Her feet were so small and plump. I would hold them in my hands and cuddle them.

It seemed as though I was drowning in the sea of my woes. My mind was numbed. I could not think about anything beyond the deaths of the two people I held very dear. It felt as though my life had come to a standstill. There seemed to be no point in moving forward.

I would awaken with thoughts of my Mum and daughter, and they would be the last thing on my mind before I fell asleep. So, the days were spent in a daze, not knowing how to pick myself up.

'Life goes on,' they say. But in all truth, life literally stops when a loved one dies. All I could see were loose ends, the things

left undone, and the things left unsaid. There was so much I wanted to teach my daughter, so much I wanted to share with my Mum. The little things that we never made time for.

The pain of losing two of the closest relations was unending. I don't think I will ever stop grieving their deaths. They will always hold a special place in my heart; they are irreplaceable gems.

I knew I couldn't go on like this, but perhaps there is a right time for everything. And the time for me to pick myself up and move on would come at its own pace. It's not that I was wallowing in misery or self-pity. I was truly aggrieved. I experienced a whirlwind of emotions ranging from stark sadness to deep depression.

There were days I couldn't get out of bed because my heart was too heavy, and my mind was numb with all the pain. Sadness ate me to my core. The days were bad, but the nights were worse. I would spend night after night crying into the darkness of my pillow.

I could not come to terms with the death of my daughter and my mother. Sometimes I would wake up hoping to hear my baby crying or to see my mother near my bedside. I could only imagine what my baby's cry was like, for our daughter couldn't cry as she was on a ventilator. So, we never got to hear her voice.

I was in a state of denial. How could it be that my Mum was no more? Why did my baby have to be taken away from me so soon?

The loss of a loved one is perhaps the worst trauma one could face in their life. And imagine losing two of your dearest loved ones one after the other. Saying that I was traumatised is perhaps an understatement. I was devastated beyond all extents. My world had come crashing down. It was as though an earthquake had hit my life and brought everything to shambles.

I felt as though I had no purpose in life now. These were difficult and trying times for me, but God is gracious. As I grieved, I began to realise how blessed I was to have received the love of my mother for all the years she had lived and how lucky I was to have held my daughter in my arms and cuddled her to my heart's content.

When someone passes away, they don't really die; they stay alive in your memories unless we forget them. There was no way I could forget my baby or my mother. To me, they are eternal in my memories, and I cherish each moment that I spent with them.

After the passing away of my daughter and mother, the reality of my life is the immense pain I experienced. Such pain can only drive a person towards depression. I was practically dysfunctional for quite a while, as their passing had left me raw, vulnerable, and debilitated.

My husband is my rock, and he has held me up and watched me fall. He has fallen with me. Without him, I wouldn't have continued after losing Mum and our daughter. He became the anchor that I held on to for security and stability. His presence in my life was the balm I needed to soothe my aching soul. My husband is my everything-in-one now, and he makes me live. If it weren't for him, I might have found life to be completely pointless.

Each day is tough, from waking up to sleeping. Mum was my best friend too, and we did almost everything together. I still re-live the day she became unwell due to COVID-19 to the day she was taken from us. I felt as though the days were passing with me in a daze. I was physically present, but my mind was so numb that I felt I was lost in a dark abyss. I still can't believe what we had faced. I am still in denial; I cannot believe that my loved ones were swept away from my life like tides sweep away debris from the shore.

The toughest days of my entire life were those when I would speak to Mum via video call as she lay there on a ventilator. I would speak to her, tell her to wake up, and try to reinforce that she could do this.

I don't know how I am coping, but I am. I have my downfalls daily... Getting by the days is a struggle.

I often stand and watch the sunset, observing how darkness takes over the night. I felt my life was akin to the sunset, from having family members who were the light of my life to the darkness of having lost them. I feel that just as the sun rises again the next morning, perhaps I, too, must learn to move on.